Edmund Hodgson Yates

My Enemy´s Daughter

A Novel. Vol. 2

Edmund Hodgson Yates

My Enemy´s Daughter
A Novel. Vol. 2

ISBN/EAN: 9783337213701

Printed in Europe, USA, Canada, Australia, Japan

Cover: Foto ©Andreas Hilbeck / pixelio.de

More available books at **www.hansebooks.com**

MY ENEMY'S DAUGHTER.

A Novel.

By JUSTIN McCARTHY,

AUTHOR OF "PAUL MASSIE," "THE WATERDALE NEIGHBOURS," ETC.

IN THREE VOLUMES.

VOL. II.

LONDON:

TINSLEY BROTHERS, 18 CATHERINE ST., STRAND.

1869.

CONTENTS OF VOL. II.

———+‡✖‡+·——

MY ENEMY'S DAUGHTER.

CHAPTER I.

AN ODD INTERVIEW AND AN UNEXPECTED MEETING.

ARE there any poor people who never felt an impress of something like awe and timidity at their first direct contact with wealth? I have heard and read of noble, independent beings, serene in the unsurpassed and conscious dignity of mere manhood, who, in whatever poverty, never felt the faintest flutter of envy, awe, or humiliation when they stood for the first time in the presence of a great man's flunkys, and asked to see the great man himself. Are there such persons? I don't say I disbelieve in their existence, but I should like to hear, on the authority of someone more skilled than I to penetrate the secrets of human consciousness, that there really are beings of that kind before I quite believe in them. My own impression is, that civilised man or woman of humble class hardly ever yet knocked for the first time at the door of a great West-end mansion, without a beating of the heart, a mingling of awe and humiliation. It is very mean and shabby and unworthy, and so are most of our instinctive impulses, which at last we school down, or are schooled and mastered by. Deep, deep down in our civilised nature is rooted the abject homage to wealth. I almost think it begins with the wearing of clothes. I doubt whether the very next stage of civilisation after nakedness does not witness the internal growth of that servile sentiment. I think we keep singing our "A man's a man for a' that," and our "*Vilain et très-vilain*," in order to drown the feeling or exorcise it, as they play martial airs to keep up the manhood of the raw recruit. Of course we get over it sometimes; at least, thank Heaven, we do not all succumb to it wholly. I am not much of a sneak myself, and I never yet sought the patronage of a man of rank, or put myself in his way to get his nod, or bragged to my acquaintance that I had met him,—and I know that I am no whit more independent than many of my neighbours,—but I have felt the poor man's sentiment of awe for wealth ; I have done to wealth the involuntary homage of being afraid, and hearing my heart beat, as I stood in its august, unfamiliar presence. Many of my friends are people connected somehow with the world of art, and who have made their way upwards from nothing. Some of them have fine West-end houses now, of their own, and carriages, and awful footmen in livery ; but I think, if I were talking confidentially with each of them in turn over a cigar and a glass of brandy-and-water, he would frankly admit that one of the most trying moments of his life—one of the moments when he found it hardest to keep up his dignity of independent and equal manhood—was just the first time when, having knocked at some great man's door, he waited for the opening of it and the presence of the flunky.

Now I stood this Sunday morning at the door

of Mr. Lyndon, M.P., and I realised these sensations. I had come to ask no favour—to seek no patronage—to bespeak no recognition—to pave the way for no acquaintanceship. If anything, I was coming out of my regular beat of life rather to confer a favour than to solicit one; and yet I did feel that ignoble, nervous tremor which the unaccustomed presence of wealth inspires in the poor man, and which is the base image, the false coin, the bastard brother of the soul's involuntary homage to beauty and greatness. I knocked at the door, and as I waited for its opening, I felt so nervous that I grew positively ashamed of myself, and took my courage in two hands, as the French phrase goes, and remembered about a man being a man for a' that.

Mr. Lyndon, M.P., lived in a fine house in Connaught-place, looking straight into Hyde-park. One had to go up high steps to get to the door, which lent additional majesty and dread to the business. It was, as I have said, a Sunday; and as I came hither I had passed crowds of people streaming out of the doors of fashionable churches, and seen splendidly-dressed women, all velvets and satins and feathers, assisted into their carriages by footmen who carried gilded prayer-books; and I wondered whether Mr. Lyndon had been to church, and if so whether he would have come back from his worship by the time I reached his house, and whether it was a dreadful heathen-ish sort of thing, a kind of outrage upon Church and State, to ask to see such a man at all on Sun-day. To go to church, too, seemed, in presence of the splendid crowds, so necessary and becoming a part of respectability, that I felt like a social outlaw because I had not been there, and was not much in the habit of going there. My sensations were not the pangs of an awakened conscience, but the kind of feeling which goes through a man who, unshaved and with muddy boots, uncon-sciously intrudes into the midst of a well-dressed and elegant company.

When I found out Mr. Lyndon's house, I won-dered much why such a man, especially if he was in the habit of going to church, could not do something kind and substantial for his niece and his brother's wife, whose chief crime, poor thing, appeared to have been her inconvenient virtue; and why he would not at least take them out of poverty and debt and the perpetual presence of temptation. This I was thinking when the door opened, and I stood in the presence of the great man's servant.

Well, it was not so dreadful after all. I really don't think I minded it in the least after the first sound of my voice. Mr. Lyndon at home?

Yes, Mr. Lyndon is at home. The servant seemed to say by his look of cold inquiry, "What then, young man? Admitting that Mr. Lyndon is at home, which it can't be worth while concealing from you, how can the fact in any way concern *you*?"

I mildly asked if I could see him.

The man—who was civil enough, by the way—merely asked if I had an appointment; Mr. Lyndon did not usually see people unless by appointment. The pampered menial of a bloated aristocracy clearly assumed at the first glance that I was not a visitor, or friend of the family.

I added:

" Will you take in my card, and say I wish to speak a few words to Mr. Lyndon very particularly? I think he will see me."

Presently the servant came back and told me that if I would wait a few minutes Mr. Lyndon would see me. I was shown into a large, cold, handsome room, with the blinds down, and a conservatory at one side. A group of marble figures, nearly life-size, stood in front of the conservatory. They were the familiar Graces, and they were covered over with a shroud of very thick muslin; so thick, indeed, that the covering seemed put on less as a protection against dust and discoloration than as a veil to hide the nakedness of the classic women during the severely proper hours of Sunday service. I did not give much attention, however, to these marble forms; for my eyes were caught by an exquisitely-framed photograph of large size, which stood, conspicuous, on the chimney-piece. It was the likeness of Christina—once my Christina, when she was poor and obscure, and we were both happy.

"Please to walk this way, sir; Mr. Lyndon will see you."

I followed the servant across an echoing hall and into a library. At a desk in the centre, with letters and papers all about him, with Blue-books piled on the floor near his arm-chair, and on his other side a waste-paper basket overflowing with pamphlets, sat Mr. Lyndon, his eyes still fixed on some document he was reading.

He was a formal, rather handsome, close-shaven man, wearing the high stand-up collars which now are almost as rare as pigtails. His thick hair was iron-gray; his complexion was fast purpling; his eyes, when he favoured me by looking up, were much lighter than those of his brother or of Lilla —they were a cold, steely gray. I marked the rigid expression of his chin and jaw—it might have been cruelty, or it might have been stern virtue, according as you please to construe it; even in history and in action it is not always easy to distinguish the one from the other. In Mr. Lyndon's case, I could not but think that the full sensuous lips helped a little to make the decision.

This, then, was Tommy Goodboy. I am bound to say that from the very first I took a dislike to Tommy Goodboy.

Mr. Lyndon left me for some seconds *planté là* without looking at me or speaking. I was, in fact, about to open the conversation, when he suddenly looked up with an air first of irritation, then of vacancy; then he looked down at my card, which was lying before him on his desk, and at last he spoke:

"O, Mr. Temple! Yes, I recollect now. My niece did speak to me about you, and I promised her that if I could do anything—but I am sure I don't know. Why did you not come sooner— some time in the season, Mr. Temple? This is no time; and everybody is out of town; and I am leaving town myself to-morrow; and, in fact, I am very busy to-day, and hardly counted on being disturbed. I don't usually see anybody on Sundays; but as you have come—and I certainly did promise my niece to see you—"

"Excuse me, Mr. Lyndon. I have not come to remind you of your promise, or to ask any favour of you; indeed, I would accept none even if it were offered, although I feel deeply obliged to Miss Lyndon."

" To Miss Lyndon?"

" To your niece. Yes."

" O, to be sure—Lilla Lyndon, my niece. Well?"

" I don't mean to make any demand on your kindness, so far as I am concerned. I hope to be able to work my own way."

He merely bent his head, as a sort of formal acknowledgment.

" I have not come on any business of my own."

" Sent by my niece, I suppose?"

" No, Mr. Lyndon. She does not know anything about my coming here."

He looked down at his papers, and glanced at his watch. The actions were significant; they said very plainly, " If you have anything to say, say it at once, and go."

" I daresay you consider my visit an intrusion."

" Not at all. At least, that quite depends—"

"I have come about a matter which concerns you, or, at least, which I thought might possibly concern you."

He looked at me with cold surprise.

"I met lately, more than once in Dover, and here in London, a person whom I believe to be a member of your family—your brother, in fact."

He did start a little and wince as I gave him this piece of news.

"I was not aware that he had returned from abroad. Are you quite sure?"

"Quite sure; at least, he told me so. Indeed, I might have guessed the fact even without his telling me."

"Well, sir, if you formed any acquaintanceship with the person you speak of—and I gather from your manner that you did—it would be super-fluous to tell you that he is not a person whose return to England could give any pleasure to me or to any member of his family. That fact it would be idle for me to attempt to disguise. I did not know that he had returned to England, or expect his return, or desire to see him. You know, therefore, that you are the bearer of unwelcome news. The question I would ask is, why you have gratuitously taken on yourself the task of making the announcement. I suppose I need hardly say that if you are the bearer of any message, or request, or anything of that sort from the person you speak of, you could not possibly present yourself with worse credentials."

"I have no message or request, and I would not make myself the bearer of any. I assure you, Mr. Lyndon, I am no friend of your brother's. No member of his family—no, not his nearest relation—could feel less inclined for his society than I am. It is just because I think him so objectionable, and so offensive, and so reckless, that I have come here to-day."

"Well?"

"Your brother told me over and over again, before I knew his name, that he had come to England resolved to expose, and disgrace, and extort money from someone. I afterwards learned—indeed, he told me—that you are the person against whom this is to be directed."

"He means to make some disgraceful exhibition of himself, to raise some scandal, in the hope of terrifying or shaming me into buying him off?"

"He does."

"He is quite capable of that, or of anything else outrageous and—and, in fact, infamous."

"I have no doubt he is. He impressed me as being all but insane with hatred and recklessness."

"Ah! but he is not insane. It would be well for his family if he were. He is perfectly sane. Well, have you, then, come for the purpose of warning me?"

"No. Frankly, I tell you that I have not; at least, not on your own account."

"Listen to me, Mr. a—a—Temple. If you should see that person again, you may tell him that he can do his worst. I shall not buy him off —no, not by the outlay of a sixpence. It's very kind, no doubt, of you to take the trouble to come here, and all that; and of course you will understand me as expressing my sense of the obligation."

"Pray don't speak of that. I have not come out of any consideration for which you, Mr. Lyndon, personally have any reason to feel obliged. But—"

My speech was cut short by the entrance of the servant, who handed a card to his master. Mr. Lyndon looked at it, and said with emphasis: "Certainly. Let him wait; I shall be disengaged in less than one minute."

There was no mistaking this. I must come to the point, and make good use of my time.

"Mr. Lyndon, I have come quite of my own accord, and perhaps very foolishly, to ask you whether you would not do something in this unpleasant business for the sake of your niece. It is such a pity that a girl so young, and so poor, and —and—" I blurted out—"so pretty, should be liable to be tormented and disgraced by a man of that kind. Could you not make terms with him, and buy him off, for her sake and for her mother's? They have had so much unhappiness.and poverty; and it's such a pity for poor Lilla."

"Mr. Temple, you appear to be so intimately acquainted with the personal history of some members of my family, that I don't suppose I add anything to your stock of knowledge when I say that I have already done a good deal for my niece."

"Yes, I am quite aware of it. She has told me so often."

"And that she has no claim on me?"

"No claim but close relationship."

"That she has no claim on me except what I feel inclined to recognise. Now, I have no objection to Lilla herself; indeed, quite the contrary— I like her. But I am not going to be made the victim of all her relations. On that I am quite determined."

"If you could even take her away—to the country somewhere?"

"I am so little in the habit, Mr. Temple, of discussing my family affairs, even with members of my own family, that I really cannot fall into the way of talking them over with strangers. Will you allow me again to thank you for the trouble you have taken in coming so much out of your way."

"You, Mr. Lyndon, I have once more to say, are in no way indebted to me. I came only because

I feel an interest in your sister-in-law and your niece. I fear I have done them little good by my interference."

"You have done them, sir, neither good nor harm."

He touched the bell that stood upon his table.

I hastened out of the room, without even going through the form of a parting salutation, which, indeed, would have been thrown away upon him, as he had already busied himself in his papers with a resolute manner, as if to announce to me that he would not look up again until I had relieved him of my unwelcome presence.

I was in no pleasant mood as I crossed Hyde-park. Especially was I out of humour with myself, even more than I was with Mr. Lyndon; and as before I had seen him I felt an unreasoning dislike to him, and as now that I had seen him and spoken with him I felt a deep detestation for him, it follows that I felt somewhat bitterly towards myself. I knew that I had made a fool of myself; that I had brought humiliation on myself; and that all this had been done to no purpose, or to an

ill purpose. It takes a very brave and loyal nature
to enable a man to be content with the knowledge
that he has made a fool of himself, even when
thereby he has benefited somebody; but it is gall
and wormwood indeed to know that one has made
a fool of himself, and at the same time frustrated
instead of serving the object he wished to accom-
plish.

So I went, scowling and sullen, across the
Park, mentally girding at myself and at the loun-
gers and idlers I met in my way. I don't know
why, when a man is in a vexed and sulky humour, he immediately begins to despise his fellow-
creatures whom he may happen to meet, and to
set them down as frivolous and worthless idlers,
gilded butterflies, and so forth. I know that I
visited, mentally, the pride and insolence of Mr.
Lyndon on every creature, man and woman, who
passed me. Madame Roland in her maiden days,
when snubbed by the aristocracy of her province,
was not consumed by a fiercer flame of democratic
passion than I felt that Sunday after I had been
a victim to the insolence of the rich member of

parliament. I daresay if the people I scowled at in Hyde-park could only have known what was passing within my breast, many of them would have felt highly flattered and delighted. For the aristocrats Madame Roland detested were aristocrats. My aristocrats and pampered minions and gilded butterflies were in nine out of ten instances people very much of my own class of life, who had come out on the Sunday to see the riders and the carriages in the Row.

As I approached the Row a haughty aristocrat passed me rather closely. He was walking, like myself. It was like his insolence and the arrogance of his class! It was his affectation of indifference to saddle or carriage-cushion. He was a tall and, as well as I could see in a passing scowl, a handsome aristocrat. I flung upon him a glance of scorn. He eyed me rather curiously; he even turned back and looked steadily after me when he had passed. I too turned, and glared defiantly at him. He was, as I said, tall—fully six feet high, I should say, with square, broad shoulders; he was dark-haired, and had a magnificent beard of curly, silky black. He was very well dressed—indeed, far too handsomely dressed for an aristocrat on a Sunday. He was not hurling back glances of scorn at me, but was scrutinising me with a grave, earnest curiosity. He advanced a step, then fell back. I too advanced, a sudden light of recognition flashing on me. Then we approached each other rapidly and at once.

"Ned Lambert!" I exclaimed.

"Mr. Banks!" said my aristocrat. It was my old friend, the basso-carpenter.

Now that I came to study his appearance, he was not changed as to features or expression. He had grown much handsomer—he always was a good-looking fellow, remarkable for his fine eyes and his beard, but now he was strikingly handsome. He was splendidly built—stately as a guardsman, supple as a gymnast. He had still the grave, modest, genial expression which was so attractive about him in the old days. He was only too well dressed; for as one came to look at him attentively, there was something about him which seemed a little out of keeping with the clothes.

Perhaps if I had not known of his origin and his bringing-up, I might never have noticed this ; as it was, I thought I could detect the outlines and the movements of the young workman under the broadcloth, the shiny hat, the fawn-coloured trousers, the lavender-kid gloves.

We were very cordial in a moment. Really it was kind of him to walk with me just there and then ; I was so very carelessly, not to say shabbily, dressed. My old friend did not seem to care.

" You have been in London long, Mr. Banks ?" asked Lambert.

I told him how many years.

" So long, and we never met all that time ! I've been away a good deal; but still it is odd that we should both have been knocking about London so much and never met."

He soon told me all about himself. He was an organ-builder, and was holding a very good position in a great house. He had himself invented and introduced some improvements into the construction of the instrument; and though these were not important enough to bring him fame or money, yet they gave him consideration with his employers and their patrons; and he looked forward to an ultimate, perhaps not a very distant, partnership. He had been sent to many foreign cities to represent his principal, and super-intend the building and putting up, the repairing and improving, of organs. He had been to the United States; he had been in St. Petersburg, and Moscow, and Stockholm; he was quite familiar with Rome, and Paris, and Madrid. He had lived ever so many lives, while I had been vegetating by the Lethean wharf of the Thames's stodgy banks. I felt myself very small indeed as he talked to me. For me, my story was told in two words: *Me voici.*

There was one subject we both seemed to avoid, yet surely we both were anxious to approach it. We sometimes beat about it; in this way, for example:

"You have been in London all lately—for the most part, I mean, Mr. Banks?"

"For the most part, yes. No, though; I was in the provinces a good deal all the summer."

"But you were in town some part of the season—of the opera season?"

"Some part of it; not lately. I only came
back to town a few days ago."

He wanted to know if I knew all about Christina. But I shrank back as yet. It came on in
another way. He insisted that I must go and
dine with him. He lived out St. John's-wood way.

"Are you married, Lambert?"

"No." He spoke very slowly. "No, Mr.
Banks, I am not married, and I am not likely to
be. I don't see what I want marrying. And
you—perhaps you are married?"

"No; I may take up your own words—I am
not married, Ned Lambert, and I am not likely
to be. I don't see what I want marrying. And
you know the reason why."

"Ah!" He breathed hard, looked at me with
a stolen glance of kindness, curiosity, and pity;
but he said no more.

"Have you seen *her*, Lambert?" I broke out
at last, and I drew him aside under a clump of
trees. "Have you seen her?"

I did not name her name—what need to pronounce it ?

"Yes ; O yes, I've seen her."

" Lately ?"

" Lately, and before, and always, I may say ;
at least, often."

"You have been seeing her—you have been
meeting her all this time ?"

" Yes; off and on, that is.   When I could,
and where I could."

Almost a cry of agony and anger escaped from
my lips.   All this time, all these years, while I
had been groping in the desolation of solitude
and darkness, he had known of her whereabouts,
had watched her, and spoken with her, and been
familiar with her !   And faithfully served her, no
doubt !   I suppose the fierce light of jealousy and
anger flamed in my eyes, for he at once said,
gently and firmly :

"For what I think you mean, Mr. Banks, it
was little good to me to see her and speak to her.
I tell you honestly, and like a man, I did my very
best to make her love me; and I couldn't succeed.

I tell you too, I was mean enough to try to serve her and help her when she wanted help, and to hope to work on her gratitude in that way; and it was of no use. She told me so at last; and then I tried to make up my mind as a man to be her friend, and no more; and I have been trying, and I think I've been succeeding even; and I fancy I'm growing better, and able to bear it, and to think of her only as a friend. Now I'll not deny that this meeting with you, and bringing back the old times, and talking of her with *you*, may have thrown me back a little. But I'll get up again, please God, and get over it. I'm determined to get over it, and to be satisfied and happy to be her friend. So you need not feel anything like anger at *me*. I have done you no harm, and myself no good."

Need I deny that a glow of wild and futile delight passed through me? It passed soon away: Lambert's ill-success was but little gain to me.

"You say you have always been seeing her; where, for instance?"

"In London, here, first of all; and in Paris,

and in Milan, and in Russia. And Paris again, when she made her great success there. And here, the other day, when she came out and carried all before her. *I* was there. I hoped to be able to throw her her first bouquet; but, good Lord, there was such a shower of bouquets that mine must have been lost among them!"

"One word, Lambert. Did she never—did she never speak—of me?"

"Not much; very little indeed. I didn't ask her any questions. I didn't know how you came to be separated, and I don't know now; and I don't ask you, either, anything about it. I tell you, however, that I thought badly of you at first; but afterwards I thought I must have done you wrong."

"Why, Lambert, why?"

"Because, from some words she once let fall, I thought she had made up her mind not to let anything stand between her and success on the stage; and I thought—although she never hinted such a thing in the least—I thought—well, I don't quite like to say it."

"Speak it out, man! Nothing that can be said by any human creature can hurt me more."

"Well, I thought she had thrown you over."

"So she did, Lambert. She threw me over, as you say—she left me suddenly. I never knew why; and I have never seen her since. I ought to hate her and curse her, and I cannot."

"No, no, you ought not to hate her. I don't understand her—I never quite could; but if I know anything about her, and if she ever loved anyone, I think she loved you."

"Did she not speak of me lately—when last she was here?"

"Yes, she did; that was, indeed, almost the only time. I went to see her up in Jermyn-street just the day before she left, and she asked me if I knew that you were living in London; and of course I didn't know; how could I? London is the grave of provincial friendships."

"Well, and she—"

"She told me you were living in London, and that she believed you were very happy."

"And did she so calmly, so readily believe

that I was happy? Did she cast me from her mind without a word of regret?"

" No, not without a word of regret; at least, I ought not to say regret, perhaps, for she said she was glad that you were happy."

" O God !"

" And she said I might perhaps meet you after she was gone, and if I did, to give you her remembrances and her good wishes."

" That was all ?"

" That was all—all she said, at least. I know what I thought at the time."

" Tell me what you thought. Don't spare me, Lambert; tell me anything—all."

" Then I'll tell you what I thought. I saw how pale she grew, and heard how her voice quivered, and I envied you; for I thought, 'For all that's come and gone, whatever is the reason of the separation, she thinks of him and loves him still.' "

" No, Lambert, you are mistaken ; you do not understand her. No, shé never loved me—never. She never cared a rush for me compared with her ambition. She despises me now because I have come to nothing so far. She pities me, I daresay, and would fling me an alms if she might; but she rejoices that she had the good sense and the good fortune to free herself from me."

Lambert shook his head.

"I don't quite understand her," he said; "but somehow I think I understand her better than you do. I know well enough how ambitious she is, and fond of admiration and applause and success, and all that; and how proud she is of having pushed her way up and up, from being a poor little girl unknown to be the star that she is. I don't think she would let anything stand in the way of her success much. But you know as well as I that human nature sounds more than one stop; and *hers* has many. And I think there is much love in her heart too, as I know there is much friendship; and I don't believe she has ever forgotten you or ceased to love you. There, it costs me something, I can tell you, to speak these words, and I shall have to smoke away very fiercely for half the night to get over this; but I think it's true. I don't know that it's any good telling you, either; for, mind, I don't say that it could come to anything now, even if you were to meet her."

" No, it could come to nothing. Don't think me an idle braggart or a fool, Lambert, or that I am talking after the fashion of the fox and the grapes; but if she stood there and held out her hand to me, and—and—offered to marry me, I would turn away from her and leave her. I would, though I love her now as much as ever—ay, far more than ever."

Lambert again shook his head, and smiled— a melancholy smile.

" No, you wouldn't," he said. " If she stood at the other side of that pathway, and held out her hand and beckoned you to come, you'd come if all the promises and vows and vengeances, and saints and angels and devils, held you back. I know that *I* would, and couldn't help myself; and I know that you would too."

" It will never be tried, Lambert."

" No, it will never be tried. She has gone away for a good long time; she told me that no matter what offers she might get, she would not come to London next season. She was thinking of going to the States and South America; they are very greedy of new singers now in Brazil. And before she comes back, we don't know what may have happened."

" She will probably marry."

" Perhaps. And you may have recovered, and may be married too."

" No; whatever may be possible, that is not. A word or two more, Lambert. Did you know of anyone who seemed likely to marry her ?"

"Likely, no; would have liked to marry, yes. No doubt the number of candidates will begin to increase considerably now."

" Ay, I daresay it will. Did you know any Italian, any musical man, who took her up, and helped to bring her out, and who was fond of her ?"

" I didn't know him; but she often told me of him. It was he to whom she owes much of her success; so she says, at least; but I don't think much of that, for her voice and her talents would have won their way some time or other. But I believe he made the way very smooth for her in the beginning, and quite took her under his care, and was better to her than many brothers or fathers could have been. She always speaks of him with great regard; in fact, with a sort of devotion."

"Was he—is he, think you, in love with her?"

"I suppose so," said Lambert slowly, and speaking rather ruefully. "Why not he as well as you and I, and all the rest of us?"

"Do you think that she—"

"No, I don't. I know what you were going to ask, and I really don't. I am sure she is very much attached to him, you know, and all that; and I don't say that if she were to marry for anything but love, she might not marry him out of pure gratitude. But when I spoke to her once about him, she was a little angry at first, and said I ought to know better; and then she softened and smiled, and went on to say that in any case his heart had two great loves already—music and Italian revolution, and there was no place left in it for any woman."

" He is older than she is ?"

" Yes; I should say ten or a dozen years at least. But that's nothing, you know; he is not old enough to be her father."

Lambert had a painfully direct and honest way of extinguishing any hope which he might perchance have lighted. I winced under his last few simple and practical words. Another point I was anxious to be informed upon.

" Tell me, Lambert, do you know anybody named Lyndon, who knows her ?"

" Lyndon, the member for Laceham, the man who lives over in Connaught-place there ? Yes, of course I know him; that is, I know all about him. In fact, I know him in the way of my own business, and I have heard of him through her."

" I don't mean him, though I am interested in knowing something about him too. I mean another Lyndon, who knows *her*, and says he helped her forward at the beginning."

(Christina's name had never once been mentioned in our conversation. We only spoke of *her*.)

Lambert shook his head.

"No, I don't know any other Lyndon but the one; and I don't like him. He is a purse-proud, self-conceited, egotistic, unscrupulous man. He has all the proud airs of a born swell, though his father, I hear, made his money in the pork trade at the time of the French war."

"But he was, and is, very friendly to *her*?"

"Yes, he was and is. I don't like his friend-ship—I suppose it is because I don't like *him*; but I hate to hear of his being near her."

"Well, that is not the man I mean. The Lyndon I speak of helped in some way, or says he did, to introduce her first to the Italian you have told me of; and he wrote to her lately, or says he did, for some money, and she sent it."

"O, *that* fellow? Yes, there is such a fellow: I believe he did, quite in a chance sort of way, meet her long ago, and he was a sort of musical jackal whom the Italian employed to discover fresh and promising voices for him; and in that way he introduced them. Yes, he did write her a beg-ging-letter lately, and she sent him money—with a liberal hand, I daresay. He is an unfortunate scoundrel, I believe. But *his* name is not Lyndon."

"He told me it was; and I believe, in that one instance, he spoke the truth."

"Perhaps so. But it certainly is not the name he went by—that she knew him by. He is a sort of fellow who probably has a whole stock of names, a perfect assortment to choose from."

We said no more on the subject then. I walked with Lambert to St. John's-wood, where he lived. A beggar would have been interesting to me just now if he came from my old home, and was in any way associated with my old life; and Ned Lambert I had always liked since the time of our memorable battle on the strand, that dark night when, falling and fainting, I awoke with my head in Christina's lap. We were, somehow, rowing in the same boat too, and were no longer rivals. Life seemed brighter for me now that I had met him. Since I came to London, seven or eight years ago, I had never spoken with or even seen anyone who came from the old home. That

whole passage of my life seemed gone and dead.
A great sea had risen up and swallowed the green,
delicious island under whose palm-trees I had sat
happy and idle so long.   It was a strange delight
now, on this hard gray shore, to meet at length
with one who, like me, was once a tenant of the
lost home.   I felt that I must be Lambert's
friend.

His manner seemed to return the feeling.   He
was always rather a diffident sort of fellow, slow of
speech, and he had not much changed in that re-
spect.   Indeed, I noticed one peculiarity about
him which rather added to his natural diffidence
and slowness of speech.   He was conscious of his
want of early education, at least in manner and
speech, and he was always on the watch to correct
any error of tongue, or to prevent himself from
making any.   Therefore he pronounced every word
slowly and cautiously, somewhat after the manner
of a foreigner feeling his way into our language;
and he lingered with a slight emphasis over words
which an uneducated man would be likely to pronounce incorrectly, as if in order to leave no doubt

that he was pronouncing them correctly. Sometimes he went a little wrong in an aspirate or an
" r," and I observed that when he did so he always
went back deliberately over the word and said it
correctly, as one brings a horse up to a fence again
and makes him go clean over it when he has failed
in jumping it properly the first time. He was
always fond of reading and thinking; when a
mere young carpenter his stock of book-knowledge
seemed wonderfully out of proportion with his
class and his manner. Now he had added to
this, and doubtless to new stores of reading gathered since, all the vast and varied experiences
accumulated during travel through many countries
by a keen, observant eye, and a robust, intelligent
mind. I could see easily enough through his
simple, modest pride in his own advancement and
experiences. I could see clearly that, in his quiet,
manly way, he was resolved on being a gentleman
in appearance and manner, as he surely was in
mind, and that he was training himself for the
task. There was so much about him that was
strong and self-reliant, that this little trait of

weakness or vanity was a softening, childlike peculiarity which made one like the man all the better.

Some thought of this kind made me fancy that
it would rather please Lambert if I were to make
a slight allusion to his improved position and
changed appearance, and I took occasion to remark on the fact of my not having recognised him
at once when we met.

"Do you know, Lambert, that I was rather
in a cynical and fiercely-democratic mood when I
passed you, and I positively scowled at you, believing you to be a bloated aristocrat?"

"No; did you, though?" he replied, blushing
over his dark face like a great girl.

"Positively I did. Did you not see my scowl?"

"Yes; I did notice somebody looking rather
sharply and oddly at me. That first attracted my
attention. Then I looked, and I recognised you
at once. But you did not seem to know me, or to
be inclined to recognise me."

"How could I recognise you at once? You
have grown such a swell."

"Have I really? Did I really look at all like

—well, like what people call a gentleman? You may laugh at me if you like; but I should very much wish you to tell me the truth."

"As I have told you, I scowled at you as you passed, out of my detestation for born aristocrats."

"Poor born aristocrats!" said Lambert, smiling, "their privileges of birth don't seem of much use when fellows like me could be mistaken, even for a moment, for one of them. Do you know that I am silly enough to be gratified when you tell me of the mistake, although I know very well that the second glance showed you what an error it was? But I don't think it's any shame for a man to try to educate himself in manner, and I am always trying it. It was a dreadful task at first. When I got to know a few people, and became noticed a little as a man who had some new notions about organ-building and all that, and one or two really great musicians were very kind and friendly to me, it used to be a dreadful trial to have to observe how people came into a room, and sat and talked, and used their knives and forks at dinner, and drank the right wine out of the right glass, and all the rest of it. The first time I went to an evening party in a white tie and a dress-coat was an agony, I can tell you. And then to have to watch one's *h*'s and *r*'s all the time did so intensify the misery. For a long time I acquired a positive reputation for sententiousness because I used to plan out little remarks and replies which should say as much as possible in the fewest words, and should have none of the dangerous words in them. I am getting better now, I think. But to this hour I am afraid of that cursed letter *h;* and when I find that I must encounter it, I fall back and have a look at it mentally first, so as to be quite sure that I know what to do with it. Do you know that I feel infinitely more happy and at my ease talking French on the Continent, or with foreigners here, than speaking English with Englishmen? Because, you know, a wrong accent, or even a slip of grammar, isn't anything with an Englishman speaking French, but it does so stamp an Englishman talking English. And I am so conscious of my own defects."

"Far too conscious, Lambert; never mind

your defects. It may comfort you to hear that I
know a man, a literary man and a scholar, too—to
be sure, he is an Irishman—who says that he
never yet met or heard an Englishman who did
not, some time or other, go wrong with his *h*, or
sound an *r* where the cynical letter had no business to come."

"Ah, but there are degrees. There's an almost
imperceptible lapse made once in a twelvemonth,
and there's a blunder that would be always coming
out if one didn't keep close watch over it. No;
you don't know what it is never to have been at
school, never to have been taught when young how
to pronounce a word, or enter a room, or properly
handle a knife and fork. Teaching oneself Latin,
or even Greek, is comparatively easy—I've done
something that way; but studying the ways of
polite society alone out of a printed book of etiquette is cruel work;" and Lambert laughed
genially.

"Then you shall teach it all to me, Lambert,
now that you have mastered the art, for I fear I
never could grapple with it alone."

"No; *you* don't want it. With you it's quite different, for you have been at school, and you have always been mixing with people. You have no idea how different is the case of a fellow who goes into anything like society for the first time, and finds himself new to the very clothes he wears, not to speak of the ways of the people he meets. I wonder a man ever has the perseverance to go through with it. Many a time I thought it really was not worth the labour and trouble. But I suppose it's something like cigar-smoking—it's sickening at first, and it takes a long practice before one can get quite used to it and enjoy it; but at last one suddenly finds he can't do without it."

Talking this way, we reached pleasant St. John's-wood, and the house in which Lambert lived. It was a pretty, fantastic little house, one of a terrace which stood upon the sort of almost imperceptible rise that in the suburbs of London men call a hill. Lambert had the first-floor of the house, and enjoyed a very pretty view over the outskirts of London; the windows being so placed as not to overlook the vast cluster of streets and

spires and domes, fog-surmounted, which lay below.   Looking from the room, one might at times
catch faint, hazy glimpses of something like the
country.   Flowers in profusion grew on the patches
of garden in front and back of the house; trailing
plants fell from eaves to basement.   It was altogether a very pleasant, gracious, and tempting
place, and I thought Lambert might well feel glad
to return to such a nest every evening from the
town.

The rooms were neatly furnished; for the most
part, of course, the regular furniture—chimney-
glass, ornaments, pictures—of suburban lodgings
in London.   But there was a small organ, hardly
bigger than a piano, of my friend's own design
and construction, with some of his special and
newest improvements; and there were some clever
specimens of wood-carving, which he made a fre-
quent recreation, he told me; and there were
books of his own—books on carving, on music, on
science, Greek Lexicons and class-books; and
there was a photograph over the chimney-piece
which caught my eye the moment I went into the

room : it was that of Christina. Lambert took a book—a sort of scrap-book, apparently—out of a drawer of his writing-desk, and, turning hastily over its leaves, called my attention to it.

" Critiques of *her*," he said ; "I used to watch for them in the papers, and cut them out and paste them in."

Yes; there were criticisms of her performances from the *Moniteur*, and the *Débats*, and the *Indépendance Belge*, and the *National-Zeitung* of Berlin, and the *Ost-Deutsche Post* of Vienna, the *Pungolo* of Milan, the *Osservatore* of Rome, the *Opinione* of Turin, the *Courrier Russe*, the *Times*, the *Morning Chronicle* (there *was* a *Morning Chronicle* then), the *Morning Post*, and I know not what other papers. I glanced over them. Often, indeed, the letters danced and flickered before my eyes. I read them with amazement, with pride, with delight—ah, and with selfish shame and pain as well! They differed as to minor points of criticism — some extolling as a special charm what others deprecated as the one sole defect; some declaring that the voice was incomparable, but the singer had yet much to learn; others insisting that the skill of the musician conquered some vocal defects; others, again, leaning more on the acting than on the singing. But all rang to the one grand chime—success. In Berlin the students of the university had a serenade by torchlight in honour of their gifted countrywoman; in enthusiastic and music-mad St. Petersburg the singer was presented, on the occasion of her last performance, with a coronet of gold and a diamond brooch. So on. It was simply success. Christina had succeeded.

I put the book away, and sat thinking and silent for a few moments. The whole thing was unreal to me; I was as one who dreams. Only the other day it seemed when she called to me a farewell from her window, and the flower she had worn in her bosom fell on the pavement at my feet.

I rose and went to the chimney-piece, and looked calmly at her portrait. She had developed, but not much changed. The photograph made her look a little older, perhaps,

than I could have expected; but most photo-
graphs have that sort of effect. She was certainly very beautiful, and of a beauty which was
in no sense commonplace. In a portrait-gallery
filled with the pictures of handsome women—
most of them even of handsomer women—one
must, I thought, be attracted at once by that
striking face, with its fleece of fair hair and its
eyes so large and dark, and the singular softness
and sweetness—almost a sensuous sweetness—of
the expression on the lips and the outlines of
cheek and chin, contrasting as strangely as did
the hue of the hair and eyes with the energy and
decision which the forehead and brows expressed.

I looked at it long and silently, compressing
my lips the while, and crushing, with such force
of self-control as I could command, all rising
emotion down into obedience. But I might have
allowed my feelings their full sway without fear
of observation, for Lambert had quietly left the
room the moment he saw me approach the photograph. He did not return for some minutes. I
conjectured that he would not return, in fact,

until I had given some audible intimation that I
needed no longer to be alone. I sat down and
played a few random chords on his organ. He
presently came in, looking animated and cheerful,
and told me he must apologise for having left me,
but that he had been compelled to have a long
and profound consultation with his landlady on
the subject of dinner. Dinner came at last, and
we drank some wine, and became very talkative
and cordial and friendly. By a sort of silent
agreement we avoided all reference to past times,
and said no more of *her*.

After dinner we opened the windows, lighted
cigars, and smoked. Lambert told me, with the
innocent, boyish pride which was rather an attractive part of his character, that he was the
only lodger ever allowed to smoke in that sacred
room; that the landlady, a most respectable old
lady, positively insisted that he must have his
cigar there whenever he pleased; and that, whenever he was leaving the place for good, he meant
to present her with a set of entirely new curtains.

"It wouldn't be any use my giving them before," he added; "I should only spoil them, and she would benefit nothing by the transaction."

The evening was calm and sultry, as we sat quietly smoking. Presently I saw Lambert get up and grasp the collar of his coat with one hand, while he looked inquiringly at me.

"Would you mind," he asked, "if I were to—" and he stopped.

"Mind what?" I asked in my turn, not having the least idea of what he meant.

"Well, just to pull-off my coat, you know. It's very hot this evening, and the fact is I haven't got rid of all the old ways yet. It does seem so pleasant still to sit of a Sunday evening in one's shirt-sleeves. I am gradually breaking myself of the fashion; but just now I begin to feel so very comfortable that, if you really *didn't* mind and wouldn't be at all offended—I have a dressing-gown, you know, and rather a handsome one; but still it isn't quite the same thing, just yet."

I could not help laughing; but he was quite grave and earnest.

" Sit in your shirt-sleeves, by all means, Lambert, if it makes you comfortable," I said. " My
poor father was a boat-builder, as you know, in
his best days, and he always used to like to sit in
his shirt-sleeves of a Sunday evening ; but I think
my mother discouraged and finally abolished the
practice in him, and she never allowed me even to
attempt it. Therefore I have an enjoyment the
less, you see, and I rather envy you your additional comfort."

So Lambert pulled-off his coat, and lay with
his lithe, long, manly figure back in his arm-chair,
and chatted with additional freedom and fluency
all the evening.

The night passed pleasantly, and it was time
for me to go. Ned insisted on walking part of the
way with me, and did in fact walk nearly all the
way. We made arrangements, of course, to meet
again, and meet often. He inquired gently and
cautiously into my prospects, and hinted in the
most delicate manner that he might perhaps be
able to give me some advice, or to make me acquainted with somebody whose advice would be

better than his. I opened to him freely whatever plans, prospects, and hopes I had.

"One thing," I said, " I am resolved on, Lambert. I will make a way and a place for myself, and in opera. I *will* be a *primo tenore* one day ; I will sing with *her*, and she shall acknowledge that I have something in me ; or I will find a way of dying, if it has to be by a plunge from Waterloo-bridge."

We shook hands and separated.

CHAPTER II.

THE HEAVY FATHER'S MISTAKE.

My parting words to Lambert expressed not too strongly a resolution which had grown up in my mind. I was resolved to slave, and strive, and wear myself out, if need be, in order to qualify myself for success in opera, that I might once sing with her, perhaps on equal terms. All other objects in life seemed to be as nothing compared with that,—thus to triumph, thus to prove myself not unworthy of the opinion she once held of me, —and then come what might!

Strangely enough, this determination was not inspired by any hope that we might fulfil the other part of our early dreams, and be married. I do not think such a hope ever entered into my ambition and my resolve. She did not love me; it was only too evident that she could not really have loved me at any time as I would have been loved; and even were it probable or possible that the far-off date of my success could find her still unmarried, I was too proud to think of courting the love of one who had flung me thus away, and left me to my loneliness and my misery. No, passionate as was my futile love for her, it was not that which now influenced me to my determination and my hopes. It was the absorbing desire to prove myself not unworthy, not all a failure. To wring that compensation from Fate was now my one sole object in life.

And if I should fail?

Well, I was no idiot, and I thought of that. The most passionate aspiration cannot conquer success, nor is it evidence of capacity for success. unless when it comes as a mere instinct of nature, like the desire of the water-fowl for the pool, of the young eagle for the flight. I therefore laid little stress on my own mere aspirations, knowing well how greatly they were stimulated by my love and my wounded pride. So I contemplated coolly the possibility, the chance, of utter failure, and I resolved upon my course. Once let it be certain, let it be beyond all doubt—and I felt convinced I could judge my own cause impartially and rightly—that I was a failure, and I would withdraw instantly and for ever from these countries, change my name, bury myself in some remote western region of America, and live there, a hewer of wood and drawer of water, till my life should come to an end.

I have said thus much in explanation of the resolute energy with which I now went to work at musical training, and at saving-up money with which to go to Italy and improve myself, and begin a career there which I hoped might wake an echo in England. My friend Lambert entered quietly, earnestly into all my plans, calmly assuming my perseverance and my success as a matter of course; and he lent me valuable assistance by advice and suggestion. Lilla, too, was in our full confidence, and was quite delighted with the project, frequently reminding me of the magnificent day at the Derby she was to have the first season of my London success. Weeks and months went on, and I began at last to see Italy in the near foreground of my hopes.

Before I proceed to sum-up in a few lines one tolerably long chapter of my life—a chapter as quiet and uneventful to tell of as it was to me momentous—I must relate two incidents.

I went very often to see Ned Lambert; he very often came to see me. He made himself very friendly and familiar with Lilla and her mother. He would sit for hours listening to the poor old woman telling him of her trials and her disappointments, her feats of cooking, her new and incomparable methods of applying sauce and preserving peaches, Lilla's sicknesses and Lilla's charms. I don't believe there was an ailment Lilla had had, from her first "thrush" to her latest toothache, of which Edward Lambert did not hear many times, and seemingly with profoundest interest, the full details. Lilla herself used to grow dreadfully impatient under these narratives, and I observed, not without curiosity and interest, that she was far less enduring now than she used to be when I was the spellbound victim.

Often, therefore—indeed, whenever I could—
I intercepted Mrs. Lyndon, flung myself in her
path, and engaged her in colloquial battle, in
order that Lambert might be saved, and that he
might, if he liked, have all the time with Lilla
to himself. I thought his eyes rested sometimes
fixedly and tenderly on her when he was not near
her, with an expression as if he would gladly be
beside her; and I was quite willing to give him
the full opportunity, so far as I could bring it
about. Soon, too, I began to observe that Mrs.
Lyndon watched with somewhat uneasy glances
when these twain talked too closely and too long
together, and that the pleasure of expatiating to
an unresisting, patient listener like myself lost
some of its charm under such circumstances.
These were symptoms, omens perhaps, not to be
overlooked.

One fine starry night of winter, when the
hardened snow gleamed glassy on the ground,
and the lighted clock of Chelsea Hospital showed
brightly through the clear and rarefied air, I
walked part of the way home with Lambert from

our quarter by the Thames. He was unusually silent for a while, then suddenly said:

"I say, Temple" (he had got into the way now of calling me Temple, and not Banks), "what a very pretty girl your friend Miss Lyndon is!"

"Very pretty, and very clever, and very good."

"Yes; she seems a sort of girl that could understand a fellow, and help him to think, and bring him out. Do you know, I talked to her just now of some new ideas I have got—good ideas, I think; in my own line, of course—and she listened to me all the time, and quite understood it all and cared about it. I know she did, by the questions she asked. Never mind the answers a girl gives. I don't; they're no test. Some girls will know by the mere expression of your face, if they haven't even been listening to a word, what kind of answers they ought to give. But the questions—if they venture upon questions, that's the real test. You can't mistake, if you have a question asked. You know at once just how far she has gone with you, and how far she is able to go. Well, sir, that girl asked me one or two questions that showed she had got rather ahead of me. She did indeed. I'm rather a slow fellow, and she seemed to make a short-cut—to cut-off the angle, you know, and get to the end directly. It must be very pleasant," he added, with a sort of half-sigh, " to have a woman for a friend—for a friend—who can understand one in that ready sort of way."

Was the inconsolable becoming consoled?

"It must be very pleasant, Lambert," I answered in deep earnestness. "It is a pleasure some of us must go without, and go darkling through life for want of it."

"She does not seem very happy there, I think," he remarked, with a nod of his head in the direction we had left.

"No. They are, as you know, very poor."

"Yes. If ever I marry, it shall be some poor girl, who will have no fortune to throw in my face, but will owe all to me. I hate the idea of benefiting by one's wife. I'd like to make my way in the world myself, and bring her along with me ; and you know I have not been doing badly so far."

"Lilla and her mother have both been very kind and good to me. I only wish I had any way of proving my friendship and gratitude."

"Is there not a ready and suitable way?"

"*Is* there? If there is, I don't know it."

"Marry Lilla." He brought out the words very slowly.

"My dear fellow, you don't know what you are talking about."

"Yes, I do; I quite understand why you cannot think of such a thing."

"No, you don't; at least, you only know part of the reason. If I had never met another woman, I should not wish to marry Lilla Lyndon. I am very fond of her, Lambert, and have good reason to be; but not in that way. My feeling in the matter, however, is not much to the purpose. Something a good deal more to the point is, that Lilla Lyndon would not marry me."

"Do you think not? Now I have often thought—"

"Because you don't know. To begin with, my prospects are all too cloudy, and I am far too poor. Lilla Lyndon does not pretend to be a heroine, and I don't believe she could be happy in poverty. She must marry somebody who can make her mother and herself comfortable, or more than merely comfortable; and I don't blame her for it."

"Yet I don't think—I am sure I am right —that she would marry for money. I think there is something better in her."

"And so do I of late. I don't believe now that she would marry for money; but I don't think she would go into married poverty—love in a garret, and that kind of thing. And I say again I don't blame her. Some people can do it, and others can't. Let us all try to understand ourselves and our capacities. One person can stand the night-air without catching cold, and another cannot; but there are some who run the risk which they might have avoided, and do catch cold, and are moping and cross about it for weeks after. Others know they cannot stand it, and take care not to try; and they are wise. Now, I suppose there are plenty of girls who

have just courage enough to take the plunge,
but not courage enough to bear the consequences
without regret and lamentation. I think Lilla
Lyndon knows that she has had enough of poverty
in her domestic life, and she has sense enough to
caution her against risking any more of it. She
is not fit for the kind of life she leads, and I
think it has gone near to spoiling her. A very
little of a better sort of existence would soon lift
her quite out of the contamination of this."

"So it would," said Lambert eagerly. He
had been listening with rather a depressed air
to my exordium against poverty.

"The fact is, Lambert, they talk dreadful rubbish about the blessings of poverty. It is all very
well for preachers and philosophers to try to gam-
mon people into making the best of a bad lot;
but there is a sort of poverty which does nothing
but degrade. All Lilla Lyndon wants, to be just
as good a girl as ever lived, is a certain income,
and ease, and no debts."

Lambert brightened, I thought, under these
words. The fact is, I began to perceive that I

had been producing, unconsciously, quite a wrong impression. When I was lecturing on the evils of poverty, I only meant to show him how certain little levities and defects had probably arisen in Lilla's character, and thus to encourage him to pay court to her, if he felt so inclined. To me he appeared quite a rising and prosperous man, and every word I used as an argument against Lilla's marrying into poverty was meant as a reason why she ought to marry him. I was fast turning match-maker out of interest in both my friends. But Lambert at first thought I was arguing against the prudence of anybody thinking of such a girl as Lilla unless he was a man of fortune, and his countenance, transparently expressive, became clouded. It cleared again as he said:

"Then you don't think she would care about a man only if he was a swell, and had plenty of money, and a house in the West-end, like her uncle, and all that?"

"No; I think she is too sensible and spirited a girl to throw away a chance of real happiness for dreams."

"You see, Temple, it's this way with me. I suppose a man can't always live alone. At least, I think now he can't; I used to fancy it would be my fate, and that it was the only thing I could endure under—in fact, under the circumstances, you know. Now, somehow, I don't think so, since I've seen that girl's bright face, and heard her pleasant laugh. And I think there's something in her too—I know it. I don't think I've fallen in love with her; perhaps I've passed the age for that sort of thing, and I've knocked about a good deal, and I'm not far off thirty years old. But I do like to be near her, and to hear her talk, and I think she could brighten a man's life very much. Then I'm getting on very well—for a fellow like me, that is, who came up from nothing; and if things don't take a wonderfully bad turn, I don't see why I shouldn't soon be able to keep my wife quite like a lady—and Lilla Lyndon would look like a lady too, and take the shine out of some of the West-enders, I can tell you."

"My dear fellow, I wish you good luck 'and God-speed with all my heart."

" Yes, that's all very fine, but we mustn't go too fast; I haven't the faintest reason to know that she would listen to a word of the kind."

" Nor I; but I don't know any reason why she shouldn't."

" Don't *you* know any reason ?"

" Not I. How should I ?"

" Unless that, perhaps—she knows you a long time, you see, and you have been a good deal to-gether, almost like brother and sister."

" Exactly, Ned; there it is—we are very much like brother and sister, and never could or would be like anything else. Lilla Lyndon has not a friend on earth who thinks more of her than I do, and I'm sure I have no friend more warm and true than she—no friend, indeed, half so warm and true. And that is all; and if Lilla should marry you, old fellow, which I sincerely hope, she and I will be just the same fast friends as ever, please God."

We parted without many more words—with-out any more words, indeed, upon this subject. But it seemed clear enough to me how things

would tend. Of Lilla's feelings on the subject
I could guess nothing as yet; but I thought it
would not be difficult soon to know all; and
meanwhile I could see no reason why she should
not love this handsome, manly, simple, successful fellow.

As for him, I envied him, because he could
love and hope. The whole thing gave me sincere
pleasure, and yet a queer, selfish shade of sadness
fell on me, too, as I walked home alone. I could
not help thinking somewhat grimly, that my condition resembled a little that of a man on board
a disabled and sinking ship, who sees the last of
his friends safely received in the boat which has
no room left for him.

That was one of the incidents I had to relate
before leaping over a few chapters of my life, because it serves to foreshadow and explain what
happened during the interval. Another incident,
seemingly unconnected with this, must be told
about the same time, as it tended towards the
same end.

One day I had made an appointment with Ned

Lambert in town. We were to meet at half-past four o'clock, and we had fixed on Palace-yard as a convenient rendezvous. It was a fine frosty evening in late February, and the cheery sunbeams were falling lovingly on the Abbey and on the gilded pinnacles of the Clock-Tower. Palace-yard was full of bustle and life; carriages and cabs were driving up every moment and depositing members, to make way for whom policemen kept scurrying here and there, and driving back the ever-encroaching rows of people who flanked the entrance to the great old Hall. I was somewhat too soon for my appointment, and I knew that Lambert would make his appearance precisely as the clock chimed the half-hour—not a minute sooner, not a minute later. So I too fell into the crowd, and occupied myself in watching the senators as they rode or drove up, and thinking what a very fine thing it must be to be one of a body of personages so high and mighty that crowds gathered to see you go to your work, and that, even though you only came up in a hansom cab, a policeman rushed to clear the way, that

your august feet might tread an unimpeded pavement. Presently, however, my eyes rested on a
figure in the little rank of spectators just before
my own, the sight of which was quite enough to
make me fall back precipitately.

It was Lyndon—the wrong Lyndon, the pro-
digal son, the outlaw. He was dressed with what
I cannot help calling studied and artistic poverty.
His hat was rusty in hue; his coat was all thread-
bare, and in one or two places actually torn; but
both were brushed with elaborate care. He had
black gloves on, which were gone in the fingers;
his trousers were strapped down carefully. Looking at him from a purely dramatic point of view,
I should say his appearance expressed Honest
Poverty in the person of a Heavy Father.

The moment I saw him I was convinced something was "up;" and I drew back to avoid being
seen by his peering black eyes. I could observe,
however, that he kept always glancing up towards
the Parliament-street end of Palace-yard.

Presently a carriage drove up, in which I saw

a face I knew. It was an open carriage, frosty though the day was. Mr. Lyndon—the Lyndon in possession, the Tommy Goodboy—sat in it, with a pale, handsome, slender young woman, whom I assumed to be one of his daughters. The carriage stopped at the entrance to Westminster Hall.

"Now," I thought to myself, "we are in for a pretty scene."

I saw the other Lyndon move forward. Suddenly he drew back, as the strident voice of the M.P. was heard saying,

"You wait there, Lilla; I'll just take my seat and come back."

The member got down and strode into the Hall, and the carriage began to withdraw to the other side of the yard.

I almost thought of profiting by the interval to seize the confounded Heavy Father, expostulate with him, and even drag him away, when I saw him break from the crowd, plunge at the carriage, and cling to its side.

"Lilla!" he exclaimed in tones so loud that

even those who were farther off than I from the carriage must have heard the words distinctly— "Lilla, my daughter, my beloved daughter! do you not know your father—your outcast, wronged father? Have they, then, taught you to hate, hate, hate me, my sweet child?—Get away, don't attempt to interfere. What business is it of yours, confound you!"

These last words were addressed to the first policeman who rushed forward and attempted to drag him away.

The young lady in the carriage sat pale and apparently bewildered, but without showing any wild affright. She was a handsome girl, with a colourless Madonna face, large deep violet eyes, and dark-brown hair.

"Come, none of this!" expostulated the policeman. "You come away quietly, or I shall have to lock you up."

"Stand back, minion! Blue-coated minion, away! That lady is my daughter. May not a father speak with his own child? I appeal to my fellow countrymen, my fellow Englishmen here around. They will not allow me to be thus ill-used."

"Bravo, old cove!" was the remark of one fellow Englishman.

"Go it, Wiggy!" bawled out another sympathiser.

The general crowd laughed.

The girl in the carriage looked paler than before, but she fixed pitying eyes on poor battling Lyndon.

"Don't hurt him," she called to the policeman in clear, firm tones. "The poor man is mad!"

"I am not mad!" screamed Lyndon. "This hair—" and he put his hand to his head, but stopped.

I do believe he was about to say, "This hair I tear is mine!" but, recollecting that he only wore a wig, he checked himself in time, and shouted, "I am not mad! That lady is my daughter."

"No, she ain't," expostulated the policeman. "I know that lady well enough. Come away now, that's a good fellow, and don't make any more row. Come away. Where do you live? where are your friends?"

"There! my daughter is my only friend. Let me go! Let me know if she casts me off.—Lilla! Are you not Lilla?"

"My name is Lilla," said the young lady, looking pityingly at him; "but I do not know you.—I am sure," she said to the policeman, "the poor man is mad. Pray take him away, but deal gently with him; and let me know, please, if you can, something about him. Send someone to me,—to Miss Lilla Lyndon, Connaught-place. Has he no friends? Does nobody know him?"

An impulse I could not resist dragged me into the business. I pushed my way through the crowd; I took off my hat to the young lady, whose sweet, calm face had attracted me from the first.

"I know him, Miss Lyndon," I said; "and if he will come with me, I shall be happy to take charge of him."

"He is mad, is he not?" she asked, bending forward and lowering her tone.

"In one sense he is indeed mad."

"Can I do anything for him? Is he an object of charity? Has he no friends?"

"He has, I believe, no friends—none whatever."

"*You* are not, then, a friend of his?"

"Indeed, no; but I know some members of his family, and should like to take charge of him for their sake."

By this time, however, Lyndon had quite recovered himself. His mistake was clear to him now. The name of Lilla had misled him. He really had thought, no doubt, that the Lilla Lyndon before him must be his own daughter. He twisted himself from the hands of the policeman, and coming up to the carriage, took off his hat and made a low bow.

"I have to ask the lady's pardon," he said, "her very humble pardon. I am not mad; I am as sane as any senator over the way, but I have made a mistake—not so great a mistake, perhaps, as it may seem just now. I am but mad north-north-west, although in this instance, and with the wind southerly, too, I have failed to know a hawk from a hernshaw. I have made a mistake, and I apologise for it. What more can a gentleman do? I *am* a gentleman, Miss Lilla Lyndon, although I confess that just at present I may not perhaps quite look like one; but you shall know the fact one day. Meanwhile, allow me again to apologise and to withdraw. Enough has been done for fame to-day. My compliments to your dear father. I decline the escort of the police-force, and I repudiate the friendship of Mr. Emanuel Temple. I want no one to take care of me but Providence."

He again made a low bow, addressed to Miss Lyndon, honoured me with a contemptuous glance, pushed his way through the grinning and wondering crowd up to a grinning and wondering driver of a hansom cab, mounted lightly into the cab, and was rattled away.

I was backing-out of the dispersing crowd too, when Miss Lyndon again leaned from her carriage, and said very earnestly, "May I ask, sir, if you can tell me anything about that strange man?"

"Nothing, Miss Lyndon; nothing that you could care to hear."

"But there is something. Pray what is his name? O, here is papa, at last."

Mr. Lyndon, M.P., came rapidly up, looking red and angry. I took advantage of his coming to escape from an embarrassing question, by bowing to the lady and walking away.

I looked calmly in Mr. Lyndon's face, but sought and made no sign of recognition. I could see that his daughter began at once eagerly talking with him, and that she glanced towards me. I could see too that he looked irritated and excited. And I had the comfort of thinking that he would probably set me down as an accomplice and actor in his brother's pleasant little performance.

The whole scene, though it seemed long, had not occupied five minutes, and the little bubble of excitement it had created in Palace-yard soon collapsed and wholly melted away.

Mr. Lyndon and his daughter drove off; and by the time Ned Lambert came up to his appointment, there was no evidence of anything unusual having happened.

I did not tell him anything about it, although I should have been glad enough of a little of his advice; but I preferred to think the matter calmly over before I took anybody, even him, into my confidence.

Late that night I was going home alone, having parted with Lambert. I was walking slowly along Piccadilly, when an arm was suddenly thrust into mine, a burst of mellow laughter pealed in my ear, and I found that the detested Lyndon was walking beside me.

"Temple," he broke out, "I forgive you. To-day I repudiated you, because I thought you wanted to disavow my acquaintance, you shabby dog, in order that you might stand well in the eyes of my pretty niece. But I am delighted to meet you now, for I do so want to talk the matter over; and you are, I give you my word, my sole confidant."

I came to a dead stand.

"Pray tell me," I asked as sternly as I could, "which is your way?"

"Just so, in order that you may go the other way. I know all about that, Temple; and, as I have had occasion to remark to you before, you sometimes adopt a sort of conventional coarseness only fit for the most inferior transpontine drama. Don't try that on, Temple. Qualify for the Adelphi, at the lowest, if you will practise stage-talk in private life. Be genial, man, be sociable! Look at me. Above all, try to be a gentleman. Don't you know that I rather like you?"

"Yes; but then I don't like you."

"Coarsely candid. *I* don't mind. Come, let us move on a little. I am going your way, wherever that is. Don't try to thwart me; I have a motive in it. I'll follow you, if I cannot have the pleasure of your friendly companionship."

It occurred to me at once that he had now perhaps resolved on changing his tactics, and persecuting his wife and child; and that he hoped, by finding out where I lived, to come upon

their track. So I straightway resolved to baffle
him. Like Morgiana observing the stranger in
the Arabian tale, I at once leaped to the conclusion that, whatever he might have in view, it
would be for the interest of society to thwart him.
So I permitted his companionship, and walked on,
resolved to lead him a pretty dance if he hoped to
find out my whereabouts.

" That was a funny mistake of mine to-day,"
he chuckled ; "but very natural. I don't know
that any harm is done, after all. It's not a bad
way of opening the campaign, and giving Tommy
Goodboy a sort of notion of what he has got to expect. What a happy evening he must have spent !
What a string of lies he must have told that fine
girl, my niece ! Isn't she a fine girl, Temple ? I
feel quite proud of her. I foresee that she will
prove immensely useful. Goodboy will have to
come to terms, or woe upon his life ! By the way,
Temple, do you know anything of astronomy ?"

" Nothing."

" Ah ! What a pity ! Then that magnificent
sky over our heads is, I suppose, all a blank to

you! Just a pavement or floor inverted! I daresay the floundering Venuses and Cupids on the Hampton-Court ceiling would interest you a good deal more than that field of sublime constellations. Well, I tell you frankly, I wouldn't be that sort of fellow, Temple, for anything you could give me. No, I wouldn't indeed; I have always noticed, though, that you professional singing-fellows are generally very stupid. The spiritual nature doesn't seem to get developed at all. Wonder how that is? The women don't appear to me to be so bad."

"Are you walking so much out of your way to philosophise on professional singers?"

"Acute youth, no, I am not. The fact is, Mr. Temple—for I want to get back to a game of billiards—I have begun to think a good deal of what you were saying, only too eloquently, the other day. It didn't impress me then, as, I am bound to say, it ought to have done. I was in a frivolous and cynical mood; unfortunately, I sometimes am so. I mean the evening that you appealed to me so very touchingly about my wife and child. You shot an arrow into the air, Temple, and, although at the moment unheeded, it came down and found its mark—a father's heart. I do now long to see my child. I thought I had found her to-day; alas! the voice of Nature guided me wrong, or at least not quite right. Temple, conduct me to my child! You know where she is. Lead me to her."

"This sort of stuff," I replied very calmly and deliberately, "does not impose upon me. I suppose you want to make your daughter the victim of some such disgraceful exposure as that to which you tried to subject your niece to-day. That you shall certainly never do by any help or hint of mine. Let that be enough. Were you to parade the streets all night by my side—to my disgust—were you to dog my footsteps for a month, you should learn nothing of your daughter from me."

"Temple, an awful thought flashes on me! I beseech of you to answer me! Heavens, it can't be! and yet—tell me, is my daughter married—and to *you*."

"She is not;" and I broke fiercely away.

" Thank Heaven for that !" was his fervent and pious exclamation.

I hurried away. He looked after me for awhile, hesitating ; then, apparently giving up the idea of forcing any more of his company on me just then, he broke into a loud laugh, sang out " Good-night, Signor Pantaloon !" and went chuckling and stamping back in the direction of his favourite Haymarket.

It was a hideous nuisance to me to have the existence of this dreadful little creature hung as a sort of mysterious burden round my neck. A secret with which I had nothing to do, which I wanted neither to keep nor to disclose, was thrust on me, and seemed to lay a sort of critical and embarrassing responsibility on me. Sometimes I thought of taking Mrs. Lyndon aside and telling her the whole matter, and so putting her on her guard; again, I turned over in my mind the propriety of trusting to Lilla's natural good sense and courage, and making her the confidante. But so long as there was any chance or possibility of his not finding them out and dis-

turbing or disgracing them, I shrank from adding
this fresh and superfluous burden of vexation to
their hard lives. It was clear that any chance
that Lilla—my Lilla—might have from the patronage or bounty of her uncle would be utterly
gone, if once her life became mixed up with that
of her unfortunate father. I very much mistook
the character of Mr. Lyndon, M.P., if that gentleman would not cast-off his niece as though she
were a plague-infected garment, once it became
apparent that recognising her would be encourag-
ing his outlaw brother. Thus far, at least, the
crusade of the latter seemed directed only against
the inhabitants of the fine house in Connaught-
place. And although I had no doubt that he
would in the end, if needful, kick with equal foot
at the door of the Chelsea lodging-house, yet,
until he showed some signs of beginning to attack, it seemed only raising a needless alarm to
put my friends on their guard.

Positively, I entertained ideas of writing to, or
waiting on, or throwing myself in the way of, Miss
Lyndon—the other Lilla Lyndon—and telling her

who the madman was, and appealing to her pity and kindliness to prevail upon her father to pension him quietly off, and thus buy his perpetual absence and silence. I fear that pure good-nature towards my friends did not wholly inspire this notion. I own that I should have dearly liked a few words of conversation with that sweet, clear voice; to have looked in those pure, pitying eyes again. Was this, then, one of the proud, cold, puritanical spinsters *my* Lilla had so often described to me? She had clearly never seen this one, at least; and, unless the latter was a very accomplished actress indeed, she could never have heard of any other Lilla Lyndon than herself. For when the little scoundrel claimed her as his daughter because her name was Lilla, her face exhibited only surprise and pity; she showed not the faintest gleam of any comprehension of his meaning or his mistake.

I could not forget her eyes and her voice. I even walked by Connaught-place several times, hoping to see her, but not confessing to myself that I did so hope. So I temporised and postponed, and kept my secret, and did nothing more. But I held still to my first impulse, and wished for a chance of trusting to the girl's pure and sympathetic face, and breaking through ceremony and conventionality by appealing to her and telling her all.

CHAPTER III.

THIS is not a story of the struggles of a poor artist and adventurer, though so much of my life was indeed just such a story. But lives like mine have been told so often before, that I could add little new by dwelling on the professional and adventurous part of my existence, even if I had the art to tell such things as other men have told them. Therefore I frankly intimated to my readers long ago that I do not mean to enter into the details of my struggles, my disappointments, my privations, my temporary success. Of all these I shall only say, like the fair dame pressed to explain the duties of the *cicisbeo*, "I beseech you to suppose them." In brief, the professional story of my life is this: I struggled long and wearily. At last I succeeded, for a time. Then

I lost the best of my voice, and I faded back into quiet obscurity, not without comfort. For what Carlyle calls four-and-twenty resplendent months, I was a brilliant success in the popular sense. I know myself, and I know that I never was or could be a great singer. I never was in the high sense an artist. I never had a genius for music, or for anything; but I had my run of success—I had my day. It was a short one, and it is over; and I don't regret it. "I cease to live," says the poet's Egmont; "but I have lived!"

In my days of swift success I came to know a great many authors, sculptors, painters, critics, artists of every class, who had all more or less succeeded in life; and I found that the actor or the singer has some splendid chances which are denied to any other adventurer after popular favour. Worst off of all his brethren I rate the literary adventurer, although Thackeray, with the complacency of recognised and triumphant genius, pointed out the immense advantage the author enjoys in requiring neither patronage nor capital, but only a few sheets of paper and a steel pen.

Where is his arena, his tribute? He has written his grand tragedy. Very good. Who is going to play it?—nay, what manager is going to read it? He has finished every chapter of his novel; and then begins the dreariest part of his business. I remember literary friends of mine used to say, when sometimes the author of *Vanity Fair* showed his grand white head among us, that he had had toil enough to persuade the public to read what he had written, that he had hawked about his great book long enough before any publisher could be induced to run the risk of printing it. The difficulty was to get any publisher to read it. Change *Vanity Fair* into a picture or a statue, and it would at least have found a place in an exhibition, where a crowd, coming for the sole purpose of looking at pictures and statues, would have seen it, and some eye would surely have found out its worth. To read through thousands on thousands of scrawled MS. pages in the hope of sometime coming on a literary treasure is a wearisome diving process which only stubborn souls long endure; but to hunt through an art-exhibition is a pleasant and easy work. I rate the chances of the painter or the sculptor, then, rather above those of the literary man. But while it is true that not everyone can get a chance of exhibiting his picture in any gallery, it is also true that even in the gallery it may pass unnoticed of the crowd, who only run to look at the pictures of men with names, or pictures they have been forewarned to look at. Suppose, however, that everyone going into the gallery were compelled to look at every picture in turn—were compelled at least to stand before it, and look at that or nothing for a certain number of minutes, would not the obscure artist's chances be immensely increased in value ? But this is precisely the condition of the actor or the singer. Once, at the very least, in his three or five acts he is in absolute possession of the audience. No one may speak or sing but he. It is his chance. If he can speak or sing in any way worth listening to, there is his opportunity of doing it. I have known scores of men in other professions who only wanted just one such chance to crown their ambition, or, at all events, to crush it, and who never got the chance, but went along through life disappointed and embittered, girding at the successful, snarling at popular favour, wailing against destiny, and always convinced that if the world could but have seen or heard them, it would have fallen in homage at their feet. The public, indeed, will not go fishing for talent, like pearl-divers. It is enough to ask that they shall recognise it when set before them. "Genius," says Mürger, "is the sun; all the world sees it. Talent is the diamond in the mine; it is prized when discovered." This was my chance. I got an opportunity of holding up my poor little artistic diamond. The opening came; I had the stage all to myself for a few moments, and I really had been gifted by Nature with a voice which then, at least, could hardly have failed to make an impression. It made its impression, and I succeeded.

This was in Italy. I came home to England, after an absence comparatively very short, a success. My way began to be clear before me. I began to have friends, admirers, rivals, detractors, satellites, partisans, and enemies. I grew familiar with my own name in print; I became accustomed to the receipt of anonymous letters—some full of praise, not a few full of love, a great many breathing contempt and detestation. I began to judge of journals and critics only according to their way of dealing with myself.

I must say that hardly any kind of life seems to be more corrupting to independent and generous manhood than that which depends upon the public admiration. It is hardly a whit better than that which hangs upon a prince's favour. The miserable jealousies, the paltry rivalries and spites, the mean, imperious triumph over somebody else's failure or humiliation, the pitiful exultation over one's own passing success, the womanish anxiety to know what is said of one, the childlike succession of exaltation and of depression, the absorbing vanity, the sickening love of praise, and the nauseous capacity for swallowing it—all these seem to be as strictly the disease and danger of artistic life as yellow fever

is of the West Indies, or dysentery of the East.
I have indeed known strong natures both in men
and women which could defy the contagion, and
retain their healthy and self-reliant simplicity to
the last. I have seen, even in stage-life, virgins
who could tread those hideous hot ploughshares of
vanity and jealousy, and come out unscathed. I
have known men who to the last kept the whiteness of their souls, and never felt a pang of mean
joy over another's failure, or of unmanly pride or
unmanly grief at success or failure of their own.
But such natures are indeed the rarest of phe-
nomena, and only make the general character of
the race show more repulsively. You can't help
it; I mean, we common natures cannot help it.
Some of us go in resolving that we will not be
like the others, that we will not lay down our
manhood and our courage and our generosity, and
succumb to the poisonous atmosphere of praise,
and rivalry, and jealousy. But we soon grow
like the rest; we rage at a disparaging word; we
swell with pride over the most outrageous praise;
our bosoms burst with gall when some new rival

is spoken of too favourably or applauded too loudly; we rejoice with a base and coward joy, which our lying lips dare not confess, when someone whom openly we call a friend makes a failure and falls down. Our nature becomes positively sexless; and man detests woman if she outshines him, just as rival beauties of a fribble season may hate each other. I protest I did not, until I came in for some little artistic success, ever believe it possible I could hate—or, indeed, that any man could hate —an attractive and pretty woman who had never either slighted or betrayed him. I soon learned that the wretched creature who lives on the favour of the public can get to envy and detest any being that stands between him and the sun of his existence.

From my soul I detest the whole thing. I distinctly saw my moral nature becoming contaminated by it, and I despised myself even for the momentary pang of pride and envy which I honestly did my best to crush and conquer. I sometimes thought to myself, " The time must soon come, if one of us does not die meanwhile, when I shall

meet Christina.   Shall I find her even as one of
these?   Shall I find that her heart swells with
pitiful pride and rankles with paltry spleen; that
she hates her rivals; that she can swallow any
amount of praise, and gladden in it ; that she can
cry when some critic disparages her or praises
someone else ?"

I could not believe it; yet I could not but
fear; I could not but sometimes wish that I had
been less fortunate in my personal ambition, and
that I were still far removed in obscurity out of
her possible path.

I heard of her often.   She was soon to return
to England, where her sudden departure and long
absence, after so sudden a success, lent new attraction to her.   People said she was married.   I had
heard the statement almost with composure.   She
had become like a dream to me.   When I saw
her last I was little more than a boy; I stood now
on the latest verge of my youth : a whole working
lifetime lay between.   I believed that I had so far
disciplined my nature and subordinated early and
disappointed passion, that I could meet her now

again with unmoved politeness, and even on our first meeting look calmly in her face, touch her hand without tremor, and congratulate her becomingly upon her great success.

Yes, they said she was married ; and it was certain that she now described herself as Madame Reichstein, not Mademoiselle Reichstein. Indeed, some maintained that she was not only a wife, but actually a widow. But they said all manner of things about her. Her husband was an *entrepreneur ;* he was an Australian adventurer ; he was a rich Yankee speculator ; he was a scion of a noble Austrian family, who never would look at him after his *mésalliance ;* whoever he was, he had deserted her : no, it was she who had run away from him while they were living at Nice, and actually in their honeymoon; he used to beat her; she once tried to stab him : at all events, he was dead now. Nay, there was not a word of truth in all that; the real fact was, that she never was married at all; the young nobleman killed himself for love of her, and left her all his property ; and so forth, and so forth. These and countless other stories—equally incoherent, extravagant, and contradictory—passed from mouth to mouth among the people I met who talked about Christina Reichstein.

I found Ned Lambert, when I returned to England, quite established as the household friend of the Lyndons. He used to come and dine with them almost every Sunday, having made a definite arrangement to that effect with Mrs. Lyndon, who was ready enough and rejoiced to eke out her housekeeping by such a mode of contribution, and who had indeed quite a genius for cookery. Lambert liked the change immensely. He said he was fond of a good dinner on Sunday, and that when he dined alone at his own lodgings, he never ventured to ask his landlady for anything beyond the cold corpse of a fowl cooked on the Saturday. But it was not his relish for a savoury little dinner which brought him all the way to our dreary district; and I saw a marked change, both in him and in Lilla, when I once more joined the little circle. Lilla was more thoughtful, more melancholy, less pleasure-loving than before; he, on the other hand, was generally brighter and more animated, unless when he was studying manners and deportment, which indeed he almost always was. Many a time I saw him furtively glance under his eyes at Lilla, as if to learn from her expression whether he had accomplished a triumph or committed a solecism of etiquette. I could not resist the temptation to make an inquiry once in Lilla's presence about his Sunday-evening relief from coat-sleeves; whereat he loked so distressed and confused that Lilla insisted on having the whole story,—and had it accordingly, and laughed very much; and Lambert at last gave way, and likewise laughed; and we all laughed a good deal longer than the story deserved. I was glad to have made Lilla laugh at anyone's expense; for, poor girl, she laughed less now than of old days, and her face looked pale and anxious. I soon found out the reason.

Between Lambert and myself we had boxes, stalls, and so forth for some theatre almost at will. One night we went—Lilla, her mother, Lambert, and myself; Lambert would not stir without Mrs. Lyndon—to see a new performer as Claude Melnotte. He, the new Claude Melnotte, was the idol of one of the colonies, and was a statuesque, handsome, deep-voiced, energetic, wooden-headed sort of actor. I thought the whole thing dreadfully tiresome, and Lambert thought so too; but Lilla was quite melted by it, and streamed with tears. A year before I know that she would have laughed at the business, or yawned over it. I saw Lambert's eyes resting on her with profound admiration and sympathy; and he looked up and caught my eye, and gave me a glance, partly whimsical, partly sentimental, partly bashful and apologetic, which would have made quite a picture in itself. She had her depths of sensibility, then, this poor girl, whose bloom the hard coarse grit of London life had so nearly rubbed away. Never did she shed tears at a theatre when I was her companion, or care for any performance which was supposed to demand tear-shedding as its tribute.

I spoke of the change to Lambert himself that night.

"It's true," he replied slowly and sententiously; "I have often thought that the best test you could have of a woman's intelligence and of her sympathies would be to watch her demeanour at a theatre. Hear her comments, and observe how she looks; and the fellow who does not know her then is an idiot, who never could know anything of her. You can't imagine, Temple, how I hate some women I see at a play : they look so cold and stolid and severely proper and self-contained, that I should like to have them expelled from the presence of art altogether. I wonder how you will feel at the sight of such people when you come on our stage, before our unimpassioned creatures here. It is not like Italy, Temple—at least, I fancy so ; and indeed I have heard it from—O, from many who have felt it."

"From Madame Reichstein, for example ?"

I was determined not to shrink from that name, or allow him to suppose that I faltered at it.

"Yes, from her in especial. She was dread

fully chilled here in London, although they gave her quite unusual honours."

"She would be. Her enthusiasm and her really lyric nature would naturally chafe against our British composure."

He glanced at me inquiringly, as if he meant to ask whether this calmness was real or put on. If I had been asked then, I could have answered in all sincerity that I believed it real. I know now that it was but an effort of self-discipline.

"We had a sort of scene at a theatre one night," he said, rapidly changing the subject; "I mean Lilla—Miss Lyndon—and I."

"Indeed! What happened?"

"Some fellow—mad, I think—seized her by the arm, just as I was handing her into a cab— her mother was already in—and jabbered some insane nonsense at her. I pushed him away, and the wretched creature flew at me like a wild-cat, and there was quite a disturbance."

"Who was he? What was he like?"

"O, quite an *outré*, mad-looking creature, small and old, with a black wig. I could have crushed him; but, of course, I wasn't going to hit a poor little old bloke—old man, I mean; and so I only dragged him away, and asked a policeman to take charge of him. But he was near raising a perfect mob about us, shrieking out that I was carrying off his long-lost daughter, and I don't know what other rubbish; and he cut my lip, so that I was a pretty sight, I can tell you."

"What became of Lilla?"

"She comported herself most bravely; neither screamed nor fainted. I got rid of my lunatic as soon as I could."

"Did Mrs. Lyndon see him?"

"No, she didn't. It so happened that she never got a glimpse of him; and I was very glad. She is a nervous woman, and would have been greatly frightened by the sight of so extraordinary a creature. Of course I made nothing of it, and I never heard any more about it."

"You never found out anything about him?"

"Never; and I never tried to."

I said no more on the subject; I needed no further explanation.

Some days after this, a few of us—Lambert, myself, and one or two rising actors and *littérateurs*—gave a little *fête* to some of our friends at Richmond. It was very early in the season. We dined, of course, at the Star and Garter. Lilla Lyndon was of the company. We were all very pleasant. I was as happy as a bright sun, delicious air, and joyous company could make any man; and I, at least, never could be insensible to the mere joy of living, of barely living, under such sun and in such air. I was a sort of rising star too, in a very small way, and might have flirted and been flattered a good deal; and did on this occasion accept my opportunities. I walked through the gardens, after dinner, with a pretty, vivacious girl leaning on my arm; a girl who had just made a brilliant success in light comedy, and promised indeed to be another Abington or Nisbett, until she married, poor thing, and died in her first confinement. Her people lived not far from Norwood; and a short time since, walking out from the Crystal Palace all ringing with music, I strayed into a church-

yard, and came upon a tombstone bearing the
name of my poor young friend.   This Richmond
day, however, of which I speak, was darkened by
no shadow from the future, and we were all very
bright and happy.

" Look there !" said my companion suddenly,
and with a joyous laugh.   " See how people make
love off the stage."

She directed my attention to two figures in a
shady little alley of shrubs and trees, not far from
us.   They were Lambert and Lilla Lyndon.   She
was leaning on his arm ; her eyes were downcast,
her cheeks were crimson, her step was slow.   He
bent his tall figure over her ; he was pleading
earnestly, passionately—that anyone could see—
into her ear.   It had come, then, just as I thought
it would.   He loved her ; and now he was telling
her so ; and I could not doubt what her answer
would be.

Queer pangs shot through me.   I was rejoiced
at the prospect of the happiness of both my
friends.   I thought with delight that Lilla would
no longer be poor ; that she would have a true

home to shelter her, a manly heart to lean on; that he would have a life made warm by love; and I longed to congratulate them both, and tell them how sincerely I gladdened in their love and their happiness. And yet the sight brought with it too a keen sense of isolation and loneliness. I had felt for Lilla just that warm and tender friendship which is to love "as the moonlight to the sunlight." She had been a friend to me when friends were most precious and most rare. She had cared for me when I was sick, confided in me always; begged for me, unasked and almost unthanked, of one who probably despised her and me only all the more for it. And now I was about to lose her; the only woman from whom I could expect a greeting that was more than formal, a glance that was at once friendly and sincere. I don't say that this made me sad. I know I was sincerely glad that things were to be so; but it made me thoughtful. I was moody enough to wish to be alone for a little; and ungallant enough to get gradually rid of my fair and joyous companion. I felt a twinge of remorse at

the recollection when I came the other day upon
the stone which bore the record of her name, her
birth, her marriage, her death, and the inconsolable grief of her afflicted husband—who is now
alive and merry with his third wife.

I was glad to be alone. I stretched myself on
the grass. The evening was glowingly, gloriously
hot. I heard the voices of singers not far away,
and the notes of a piano. I saw nothing but the
unflecked sky of blue above my head, and the
slender spiral vapour of my cigar. Was I happy?
Was I miserable ? Happy or miserable, those
moments were ecstatic. Are not the sensations
produced by extreme heat and extreme cold so
much alike that the African brought for the first
time into contact with snow fancies it has burnt
him ? I think there are pangs of delight and of
pain—where the soul is the medium, not the
nerves—which are not easily to be distinguished
from each other.

I started at an approaching step. Lilla was
close beside me ; she looked pale, and much distressed. I jumped to my feet.

"I have been looking for you everywhere," she said; "I want you to take me home."

"Home so soon? Are you going home already?"

"Yes. I should like to, very much; if you don't mind leaving so early. Or I will wait longer, as long as you like, if you will promise to leave a little before the rest, and to come with me."

"Certainly, Lilla, when you please. But where is Lambert?"

"Mr. Lambert? I don't know; at least, I saw him not long since."

"Will Lambert not wish to see you home?"

"If you can't or won't come with me, Emanuel," she said petulantly, "if you must wait on somebody else, of course I must not worry you about me."

"Why, Lilla, my dear girl, you know very well I will go with you when you please. But I only thought—"

"Dear Emanuel, please don't think anything; at least, at present. Only do oblige me this once; I am so tired, and I want to get away."

" We will go this instant."

" Thank you; that is kind. And I should like to get quietly out, quite unnoticed, if you please."

" This way, then."

" I gave her my arm, and I felt her arm tremble on mine; and could feel that her bosom beat heavily as she leaned on me. Violet circles were round her eyes; and every time she spoke it seemed as if she must break into tears.

There were several hansoms at the door, in which some of our company had come. I meant to take one of them, and convey Lilla home in it. Young ladies don't usually go in hansoms, I believe, with young men; that is, where Respectability reigns. We had no such etiquette in our free and gladsome world. One of Lilla's special delights was, or used to be, a hansom.

But the gardens were full of company. There were many parties there as well as ours. Lilla and I, threading our way outward, were always

coming on some brilliant group. It was significant of my poor young friend's state of mind, that
she did not even cast a scrutinising glance at the
dresses of the ladies. We hardly spoke at all.

I brought her into a narrow side-path between
flowers and plants. We were nearly out now.
Towards us there came a group of four or five
ladies and gentlemen, straggling along as the
width of the path allowed them. One voice struck
on my ear, and I knew its sharp and strident tone.
I knew it to be the voice of Lilla's uncle. Emi-
nently disagreeable I thought such a meeting
would be in a place so narrow that recognition
could not be avoided. It was now too late to
go back, so we drew up to let the group stream
by.

Lilla saw her uncle. She coloured, and was a
little confused. He did not seem particularly delighted at the meeting.

"Why, Lilla, *you* here?" He gave her his
hand rather coldly.

I had been standing silent and stiff, looking
at nothing and feeling highly uncomfortable.

"Yes, uncle; but I am going away now. I have asked this gentleman—don't you know Mr. Temple, uncle?—to take me home."

"Indeed! Yes.—How do you do, Mr. Temple?"

I made a formal acknowledgment of his enforced salutation, and in doing so I became conscious that the light of two deep, dark, soft eyes was turned full on me. I became conscious of it —I can use no other phrase—for up to this moment I had positively seen none of the group but Mr. Lyndon alone, and had never looked at the lady who was by his side, and who stopped when he did. But I felt that the light of those eyes was on me, and an electrical thrill ran through me, with which the blood rushed heavily and fiercely to my head, and the pulses of my heart seemed to stand still, and the grass for a moment flickered with changing colours, and the sinking sun appeared to reel in the sky.

And looking up, I saw that Christina Reichstein stood before me.

Not my Lisette! Not my Christina! Beau-

tiful, stately, in the full glow of developed loveli-
ness—no longer a girl; nay, now that the wester-
ing sunbeams fell upon her face, I saw that there
was something even of the melancholy beauty of a
sunset in her own features and expression. Far
more beautiful, far more stately, far more attractive, than when I knew her, but not with the
fresh and passionate youth which was her exquisite charm long ago. Long ago! A whole life
seemed to lie between that time and this. I
thought there was something sad, something even
of a prematurely wasted look about those glorious
eyes. Youth, and early love, and early struggle
lay buried in those lustrous hollows. They were
as mirrors to me, in which I saw my own dead
youth and disappointed love. I turned towards
her, and our eyes met and rested upon each other
in an instant of unspeakable emotion never to be
forgotten in this world.

Christina recovered her composure in a moment.

"We are fortunate, Mr. Lyndon," she said,
in her clear musical voice, with the old dash of

foreign accent still perceptible in it,—"we are fortunate in not having left so soon as I wished; for we meet—at least, I do—two unexpected friends. Your niece I know already, though she seems to have quite forgotten me; and in this gentleman I meet a very old friend."

She gave her hand first to Lilla, and then to me. Not the lightest, faintest pressure of her glove indicated to me that I was anything to her but an old acquaintance.

"Indeed," said Mr. Lyndon drily, " I did not know that you were acquainted with this—ah, this gentleman, Mr. Temple, before."

" Did you not? O yes; we were old acquaintances ever so many years ago.—How long ago, Mr. Temple ?"

"Several centuries ago at least, Madame Reichstein."

" Yes, indeed; it must be many, many centuries ago," she said, slightly shrugging her shoulders.

" A good way of evading any confession of the number of years," remarked Mr. Lyndon, with a short dry laugh.—" If you are going home, Lilla, I think you had better come with us."

" Thank you, uncle. If you can take me, I shall be very glad; and then Mr. Temple need not be dragged away to take care of me."

" No; we need not trouble Mr. Temple to leave so early. Come, Lilla."

" Good-night, Emanuel," said Lilla, holding out her hand to me. " I am so much obliged to you for offering to come with me; and so glad that I have not to take you away."

" Then I think I shall not go just yet," said Madame Reichstein. " I will go in Mrs. Levison's carriage; she is not leaving for a few minutes. I have not had the pleasure of seeing Mr. Temple for so many years that I cannot leave him now, at least until I have exchanged a few words with him, and told him how and when he may see me again.—Will you give me your arm, Mr. Temple ?"

I offered her my arm without a word. Lilla looked at us both with wondering eyes. This was all the wildest of mystery to her. She forgot for a moment apparently even the trouble that was oppressing her, in the surprise of seeing this un-expected acquaintanceship reveal itself.

"Remember you promised to accept a seat in my carriage," said Lyndon. "We are in no haste; we can wait as long as you please."

"But I don't like the idea of anybody waiting for me. No, Mr. Lyndon; pray excuse me this once. Your niece, too, looks quite tired and ill, and I think the sooner you take her out of this the better."

Lyndon scowled and contracted his brow, and looked at Lilla as if he could have found it in his heart to say something rather sharp of her illness, and her presence, and her existence altogether.

"O, Lilla's very well," he snarled.—"Are you not?"

"Quite well, uncle.—I am quite well, indeed, dear Madame Reichstein."

"You don't look so, child. No, you must go home, dear; you will come and see me, will you not? I have scolded your uncle before now for not bringing you to me. Good-night, dear." She

kissed Lilla quite affectionately.—"Good-night,
Mr. Lyndon, and thank you very much."

"Good-night. But you will be at Mrs. Levison's to-night, will you not?"

"Really, I had quite forgotten. O yes, certainly—at least, I think so. *Au revoir*, then."

Mr. Lyndon saluted *me* very slightly and
formally, and I saw him cast an appealing, disappointed, impatient glance at Christina. It was
vain, however. She bowed graciously, smiled
sweetly, and then turned and led me away.

All this time I was like one paralysed of
speech. Not even that fiercest stimulus a man's
power of self-control can receive, the consciousness that he is making himself ridiculous, could
spur me to the mastery of my feelings and the
faculty of unmeaning talk. Lately, when it had
become apparently certain that I must some time,
and that soon, meet Christina, I had rehearsed
over and over again the manner in which I should
demean myself. Sometimes it was to be a dignified and haughty coldness, sometimes an air
of polite, genial, easy indifference. But the one

way in which I was never on any account to
greet her for the first time was just that which
I now found myself driven into—confusion, em-
barrassment, constraint, and awkward silence.

My throat was dry, my lips were parched; the
trail of her rustling dress along the walk was the
only sound that seemed to reach my ears; the
fragrance of perfumes came faintly from around
her; her hand rested on my arm. I did not venture to look at her, lest I should meet her eyes,
and, stricken by them, give out my soul in some
wild outbreak of love or anger.

" Emanuel!"

The word came up low, sweet, and thrilling to
my ears. It pierced my heart. It seemed as if
between that word and the " *Ade!*" I had heard
her call from the window years and years ago there
was only an utter void.

" Emanuel!"

" Madame—Madame Reichstein.'"

" No; not that name, Emanuel. Call me by
the name you always gave me—long ago. That
at least is mine still."

" Christina !"

" Yes.   I am still Christina.   You must not think harshly of me, Emanuel."

" I do not.   Heaven knows I do not."

" You cannot judge me, and you must not attempt to do so.   I know by your manner now that you think I have injured you."

" Think you have injured me!   Think!   I look back on so many years of a life worse ten times than any death, and you wonder whether I think you have injured me!"

" Emanuel, if we begin reproaching, I too have something to reproach.   If we begin talking of years of suffering, do you think life has been all a pleasure and a joy to me?   If you were disappointed, was not I?   If you were deceived, was not I?"

" By me, Christina?   Never.   I—I—loved you, you only, and with all my soul—"

" Hush, hush, my friend, no more of that. No, not one word.   All that is dead and gone long ago.   Let it sleep.   Why should we begin raking up the past, and reproaching each other, and making each other miserable ? I did not wish or mean to do so. I wished that we should meet like old friends long separated, who are friends in heart still. I have heard of your success, Emanuel, and I congratulate you. I heard of it but now in Italy, where, look you, you have friends. Greater success too you will have yet. I was not surprised ; I always knew it. And me —look at me. Well, I have not failed."

"No. You have indeed succeeded. You, Christina, have realised your highest dreams ; you have all you ever longed or prayed for."

"And you envy me, perhaps ? And look coldly at me? And wonder why I have succeeded so much better than others ? And will join with my enemies in finding defects, and blaming the prejudiced public which overrates ? No; I do not think you would do that. That would not be like you."

" Christina, that you could even suggest it shows that you do not know me. But, indeed, you never did."

" Did I not ? But we will not talk of that.

Well, then, I have succeeded; and you are just on the verge of full success. They tell me we are to sing together soon."

" So they tell me."

" Yes, I believe so; I suppose it will be. In fact, I will have it so, although Mr. Lyndon does not seem much to like it."

" What right of judgment has he ?"

" Well, you know the right he has"—and she shrugged her shoulders—"the right of the man with the money who stands quietly in the shadow behind the manager whose name is on the bill. That right he has. But to me it matters little ; I have my own way, or——"

"Mr. Lyndon is a close friend of yours ?"

" I suppose so. I have a great many close friends, and I hope I value them all exactly as they deserve. You look coldly and strangely at me, Emanuel," she said, suddenly changing her tone of flippancy and cynicism, for the old friendly pathetic voice, " and you seem as if you too would judge me only by words, and ways, and externals. If you will, I tell you frankly beforehand that you

will judge me harshly—as, perhaps, others do—
and you will judge me wrongly, and I shall be
disappointed. Do not; O, do not! We shall
have to see each other much in the future, and
I should like dearly to have one friend and brother."

Voices were close behind us; and I heard
Madame Reichstein's name mentioned as if she
were sought for.

" This way, Emanuel, please ; I see my friends,
and I must go with them. Is it not all like a
dream that we have met again? Thank you,
Mr. Temple ; you will come and see me ?—Now,
dear Mrs. Levison.—Good-night, Mr. Temple."

She gave me her hand, and said in a lower
tone, " Good-night, Emanuel ;" and left me.

I sauntered vacuously back into the garden.
My brain was all in a whirl. I put between my
lips the cigar long since extinguished, and was
for a while unconscious that it did not burn. A
sense of disappointment mingled with all the confused feelings that came up in my mind. The
Christina I had found was not like the Christina

I had lost. Something of sharpness, of worldliness, of flippancy, seemed in her, which jarred and grated on me; and yet now and then some word or tone brought back all the old memories, the ideal Christina, the strong love. I tried to remember and dwell on only the one delicious, pathetic sound which came from her lips when she spoke my name, and to put aside all association of her with the common world—with Lyndon's coarse and purse-proud ways, with the kind of society in which Lyndon strove to be a dictator, with the paltry spites of cliques and the mean jealousies of rivals. I tried to do this; I did my best to succeed; but the sense of disappointment outlived my efforts.

CHAPTER IV.

A BREAKING-UP.

I DID not want to meet Lambert or any of my
friends any more that night; I had no motive for
wishing to be home early; I had no motive, indeed, for wishing to do anything, except to get
away from just the place where I was : so I lighted
a cigar and took to the road. I walked from Richmond, choosing all the byeways and circuitous
complicated " short-cuts" that could well be found,
so that by the time I arrived in town I was pretty
well tired. I looked into a theatre, and found it
very dull; I dropped into a small and modest
club of artists and journalists and young authors,
of which I had lately become a member, and
listened to some of the ordinary gabble in the
smoking-room, about this man's piece and that
man's novel, and this other's overdone " business"

in the comic part, and somebody else's anger at
the malignity of the critics, who don't see the
merit of his wife's novel, and all the rest of the
kind of thing which one hears in such a place.
It was weary, or I was weary, and I hardly talked
to anybody.

At last it grew late, and I went home.   I
had resolved to stay out long enough to be certain
that I should find nobody stirring; I was disappointed, however.   There were lights in the little
parlour; I let myself in with my latchkey, and
would have gone upstairs, if I could, without
seeing anybody.   As I passed the parlour-door,
however, Lilla's voice called me; I went in, and
found her looking very pale and weary and sad.
She was still in the dress she had worn that day
at Richmond.

"Not in bed yet, Lilla?"

"Not yet; I have been waiting up partly to
see you.   Mamma is up too.   I am going away
to-morrow, Emanuel."

"Going away!   Going where?"

"I am going to Paris.   I am going to have

a hand in a school there—in a kind of partnership with a person I know, a very clever sort of woman, a Miss Whitelocke, who took quite a liking to me, and has a very good opinion of my capacity—no great proof of her cleverness is that, certainly."

" But this is very sudden ; you never spoke a word to me of this before."

"No. Because nothing was certain, and I hadn't made up my mind; and we both have our secrets, Mr. Temple, have we not? You always spoke of me as your sister, Emanuel; but you seem to have kept something from me which you would not have kept from your sister, and you allowed me once to exhibit myself in a very ridiculous light."

" Lilla, my dear girl, indeed there was nothing to tell. I did not know myself who she was; who Madame—"

" I don't want to know your secrets, Emanuel, and don't look put out about it, for I am not at all angry, and I think you showed only your good sense in not trusting so silly a creature as I have always proved myself to be."

"Indeed, indeed, Lilla, you don't understand me; you can't understand why I could not be as frank with you as I could have wished to be."

"Please let us not talk any more of that just now. I am going away, Emanuel; I must go from this place. I must try to do something for my mother, and make a home for her. O, she has need of every help, and she has no one but me—no one. Everyone despises her—and us both—and I don't wonder."

"Your uncle, Lilla: does he know?"

"My uncle? Yes, he does. He scolded me to-day, and—and told me we were a disgrace to him; and so we are. And do you know what he offered, Emanuel? He offered to take me into his house and keep me like a lady—like one of his own daughters, he said—if I would leave my mother, and promise not to see her any more, except once a month, or something of that kind. My poor dear, loving, foolish old mother! She has made a slave of herself all her life for me; and little return I ever gave her."

"What did you tell him?"

"Well, I told him what he will remember.
I flashed out upon him, and told him just what
I felt; not a word did I spare. I told him I
scorned his money and his kindness, and that,
please God, I would stand by my mother while
she lived; and I am afraid I added that perhaps
some day one of his own daughters might be
invited to leave *him*, and might give a different
answer from mine. He was quite white with
anger. I didn't care—I don't care. I am glad
I spoke out; it did me good; perhaps it will do
him good."

"Lilla, I always thought you had a fine noble
nature; now I know it."

"Noble nature! nonsense. I am not going
to desert my poor mother—now especially—that's
all. But I waited up to tell you all this; and I
want you not to say anything to her about the
condition my uncle offered, for I haven't told her
that; she would worry me to death, poor soul,
about sacrificing myself, and stuff. And I want
you to back me up; to say that everything I do
is right and wise, and for the best, and all that.

You will do this, Emanuel, like a kind, dear fellow, will you not? And don't speak of anything else, anything you may know or guess, or that—O, you *must* understand me; but just tell her you think I am doing the most sensible thing possible in going to Paris."

"But, Lilla, tell me—do let me ask you— why are you doing this? Do confide in me. You may do so; I know all."

"All?" she said, flushing up.

"Yes, my dear, all. I know, for instance, what happened to-day. I knew it was coming. Now, why can you not stay and make Ned Lambert—that true-hearted, manly, clever fellow—as happy as he asks to be?"

"Emanuel, you have said you know all. If so, you know my reason. I cannot bring disgraceful vexation on Edward Lambert; and to marry me just now would bring disgrace on any man. O, I am so unhappy, so wretched; and I have been crying all the evening. I have been silly and deceived all my life through, and filled up with foolish and false notions and expectations; and at last I know the whole truth. It is enough to crush anyone." And the poor girl burst into tears.

"Have you told Lambert your reason," I asked; "the reason of your leaving London?"

"I have not, I have not; and I am ashamed to say that I have still idle pride enough left in me to conceal the truth from him."

"But really, Lilla, I must ask you—is the thing so bad as all this? Are you not far too sensitive? You can't suppose Ned Lambert could be affected for a moment in his feelings towards you by the fact that—" I stopped, rather embarrassed. What was I to say of her father? This, of course, was the obstacle and the disgrace of which she had spoken.

"No, Emanuel, I don't. Ah, I know him too well; and for that very reason I will not allow him to be victimised."

"But would you not let him judge for himself?"

"No, Emanuel, no, no. Don't speak of it to me, pray don't. And O, I beseech of you, I implore of you, don't tell him! Don't let us seem disgraceful in his eyes. Listen: I have not been brought up well, Emanuel; I need not tell you that. I have not been made to care much for truth and religion, and anything of that sort; and I am not religious, or particularly good : but somehow I never did see this so plainly as of late, when I came to contrast myself with others—and with *him.* I don't think I should have been fit for Edward Lambert at my very best. I don't think poor mother and myself are much the sort of people to make a very delightful home for so good and noble a man. But this last thing I have come to know has decided me. Emanuel, have you seen my father?"

"I have. I have known him for some time."

"And known who he was?"

"Yes, Lilla."

"Yes. And you kept it to yourself, because you did not wish to shame me?"

"No, Lilla; because I did not wish to pain you when there seemed no need of it, or no good likely to come of your knowing it. It does not shame *you;* it cannot."

"Not in your eyes, perhaps, for you know us; and you know it is no fault of ours—at least, of mine. Not in your eyes."

"Nor, surely, in *his*."

"O no, no; I know that. But it would bring on him endless vexation and humiliation; and I should be a scandal to him, even though he did not say it, or think it; and I cannot bring him or myself to such a pass. I could bring him nothing but disgrace, and that I won't bring him; I think too highly of him. I feel that I am doing right; and I think it is the first time in my life I ever resolved upon doing anything just because it was right. I have been silly and frivolous enough; but I have my feelings, Emanuel, and my sense of honour, and my pride, like other people."

"Lilla, my own," called her mother's voice from below, "it is late, my dear, and you ought to be in bed."

"Yes, mother, I daresay I ought; and accordingly I am not."

Lilla was going to make—nay, actually had

made, and in very spirited fashion too—a great
sacrifice for her mother, but she could not keep
from occasionally snubbing her. Good Mrs. Lyndon was sometimes a trying personage to a quick,
impatient young woman; indeed, she was one of
those good people who seem made to be snubbed.

She came up herself presently, looking very
shaky and flustered.

"We're going away; we're all breaking-up,
Emanuel," she said, looking inquiringly at me.
"Lilla's going in the morning."

"I know, Mrs. Lyndon."

"It seems sudden, don't it? And we were
just getting all to rights here, after such trouble
and difficulty and work. But Lilla thinks it's for
the best."

"Yes, mamma; we've argued the point already
quite enough, I think."

"She won't give in to her uncle, Emanuel;
although you know that he's been so good to
her."

"Stuff, mamma! Now do stop, there's a good
woman."

"And you've heard something else, Emanuel?
—Have you told him, Lilly?"

" O yes, mamma—yes."

" She's refused him, although he is so good
and kind, and so fond of her. Of course he is not
what I should have liked, and what I should once
have thought only right and proper for Lilla to
have. She ought to be a lady, and of course Mr.
Lambert isn't the sort of person one had a right
to expect. O dear, there was a time when, if anyone had told me that a person in his position
would have thought of asking my Lilla to marry
him, I shouldn't have thought he could be in his
senses—I shouldn't indeed! But you know, after
all, people must yield to their circumstances; and
what I say is, I never knew a better or more worthy
young man—and doing so well too. I do think
it's a pity; but Lilla's so wilful."

"I suppose I was always wilful, mamma,
wasn't I?"

" Yes, my own, that you were; and such a
troublesome girl, many a time."

"Yet you were always fond of me, you dear old woman."

"Fond of you, my love? Ah, fond is no name for it!"

"Well, then, you will continue to be fond of me still, though I am more wilful now than ever. Besides, if I was always so, it isn't much use trying to be anything else now. 'What's bred in the bone,' mother; and all the rest of it."

Lilla was doing her best to carry it lightly, saucily off. The effort was not very successful.

"Have you advised at all with Mr. Temple, Lilly?" And the mother threw an appealing glance at me.

"I have, mamma." And the daughter threw an appealing glance at me.

"Yes, Mrs. Lyndon, I have talked with Lilla. I did at first speak to her as you have done; that is, to something like the same effect. I did think she might have married poor Ned Lambert at once, instead of postponing it. But I must say that she has spoken to me in a way which shows me that she has clear and strong reasons, and a feeling

that we must not try to counteract. You must let
her have her way, Mrs. Lyndon. I think we may
trust her that she is guided right; and I hope and
believe I shall see her and you, and Ned Lambert
too, happy, quite happy, before long."

"If it please God," said Mrs. Lyndon with a
half-querulous sigh, which seemed to say that one
couldn't always rely upon Providence to do exactly
the sort of thing one wanted.

"You don't mean to see him again, Lilla?" I
said, turning back as I was about to leave them for
the night; "not in the morning, before you go?"

"O no, Emanuel; it would do no good. I
don't want him to know until after I am gone.
You will give him this little packet, please, from
me; it's only a poor little keepsake; and you
may tell him, if you like, how sorry I was for going; and you will put it in the best light you can,
and make him see that it can't be helped. And
you may tell him, if you like, of my gratitude to
him, and—and—of my unchanging love."

She fairly broke down at last into sobs, and
signed for me to leave her.

I left her with deep regret, and sympathy, and pity. I confess it seemed to me that she was making a needless and quixotic sacrifice; but from her point of view what she was doing was clearly right, and I could not but admire the quiet, resolute spirit with which she had chosen her way and walked whither it led her. I felt in this regard a thorough admiration for her. A sort of pariah myself, I always feel a special and natural pride in any brave good deed done by one of my caste. It is the business and the inheritance of the Brahmins to be brave and good, and to think no little of their own bravery and goodness; and they do not want the admiration of such as I am. But when the courage and virtue are shown by one of those from whom we do not expect anything of the kind, then I am inclined to wave my cap and cheer. We hear of all sorts of self-sacrifice in books, and even in real life; some of it of a very stony, implacable, and self-tormenting kind, which I at least cannot find it in my heart either to love or pity, but only shudder at, and pray to be kept for ever out of the presence of its silent icy rebuke

and self-assertion. Self-sacrifice is indeed the
model and pet virtue of the age ; and some of us
are always inclined to rebel against models and
pets. Moreover, it is almost always exhibited by
somebody from whom it is naturally to be expected
—the *noblesse* of whose virtue, personal and in-
herited, obliges its owner to such deeds of devotion ; it is done under the impulse of lofty religious
inspirings, it is preached up by good and author-
ised preachers, it is sanctified with holy texts, it
is illumined and encouraged by hopes of everlast-
ing reward and the eternal society of harps and
seraphs. My poor little London pagan had no such
stimulants and encouragements. Her sacrifice
was not made as a slave performs a duty, or as a
courtier denies himself now that he may have the
greater thanks hereafter. It was altogether the
impulse of native honour and nobleness and love—
above all, love. It thought of no reward, here or beyond ; it was all sacrifice. It was foolish, perhaps,
in one sense ; but there are some of us in whose
eyes even Virtue looks most attractive when she
is a little irregular and unorthodox in her ways.

CHAPTER V.

"THOU HAST IT, ALL!"

So our dreams had come true at last; our wildest
hopes had been realised. We had both succeeded.
Christina and I sang together during the remain-
der of that season at the best house. She was
the great success and idol of the hour; I was, in
my own way, a success too—greater than I had
ever expected to be. Just think of the changes
time had worked for me with unthought-of liber-
ality. Only a little while ago I was poor—horri-
bly, bitterly poor; a man to whom the fare of a
hansom was an expense to be avoided and fought
against. Now I had, for a bachelor, plenty of
money, and spent sovereigns heedlessly where
even two years ago I dared not lay out shillings.
Now I had a name that was known pretty well
everywhere—that is, where people talk about sing-

ing. Now I was once more restored to the society of Christina. We sang together; our names were constantly and of necessity coupled. I saw her almost every night. We were applauded together; I led her before the curtain at every recall; I gathered up her bouquets for her. On the stage I was always associated with her; off the stage I could see her when I pleased. We were now in very reality swimming together, and side by side —the success we used to dream of and rave about years ago.

Was ever mortal so blessed of the gods as I?

Let me answer in a sentence. My life was unhappy, and I was sinking every day in my own estimation deeper and deeper; I was becoming demoralised.

I have already said that during my long separation from Christina her memory was my preservation from anything mean or low or degrading. How did it happen that association with her now seemed to produce just the opposite effect?

To begin with, I could not any longer under-

stand either her or myself. She was no longer
my Lisette. All the freshness of her nature
appeared to have been washed away. Her soul
seemed somehow to have contracted; the brand
of the world was on her. The bloom was off her
cheek, and, as I believed, off her heart. Yet she
fascinated me as she did others; and I clung to
her, and walked in her shadow, and was unhappy
without her, and unhappy and disappointed with
her.

Except when on the stage. There, and only
there, I saw my Christina. I have avoided, and
shall avoid, a cold and lengthened description of
her as a singer and an actress. But she delighted
me, and, I could have almost said, she surprised me.
Her voice was as it had always been, more remarkable perhaps for its clear, bright, vibrating strength
than for the softer and sweeter tones; but the
great charm about her was the perfect unity and
harmony of her acting and her singing. She did
not quite belong to that grand and classical line of
singers which seems for the present to have closed
with Grisi; neither had she anything in common

with the school of the pretty musical humming-
top, the warbling butterfly, which is just now our
pet ideal. Her voice and her style expressed romantic, not classic, passion and love and tragedy.
She was always a woman ; never a goddess. But
her whole soul was infused into what she sang.
She was to the grand classic singers what Victor
Hugo is to Racine. Into mere piquancy and
prettiness she never degenerated.

I admired her greatly, wholly. In everything
she did there was the unmistakable presence of
genius. But when I strove to criticise her calmly.
putting myself into the position. as well as I could,
of the average public, and asked myself, " Will
her fame last ?" I was forced to reply, " I do not
think so."

In the first place, she was not careful of her
voice. She exerted its powers with a generous
carelessness, a splendid indiscretion. Each time
she appeared on the stage she seemed to have
said to herself, " This night I will do my very
best, no matter what my state of health or
strength : let to-morrow care for itself."

But, again, I doubted for the permanence of
her noble, natural, thrilling style in its hold on
public favour. It was not the lofty, the goddess-
like, the terrible, which made other great singers
irresistible in their power; and it had nothing to
do with the saucy fascinations and joyous little
nightingale trillings which set vulgar audiences,
no matter how high their social rank, into ecsta-
sies. There was neither terror nor trick about it.

It was difficult for me to criticise even thus
far, for I hung upon her voice and her successes
like the most devoted lover. The first time we
sang together I was almost indifferent about my
own success, so completely was I wrapped up in
hers.

On the stage, then, she was all I could have
expected, the very danger which I feared for her
coming only from the truth and integrity of her
artistic genius. But the moment she ceased to
be a lyric queen and became Christina Reichstein—I could hardly now call her, even to myself, Christina Braun—she disappointed me while
she most fascinated me. I had to go away from

her in order to bring the true Christina back into my mind.

She coquetted with anybody, everybody, who paid her homage—with, for a long time, one exception, myself. Of course I hung on to her like an idiot; I did indeed still passionately love her; but it was a long time before one glance of encouragement invited me on. Understand that this in itself was often to me a flattering and a maddening incitement. She seemed, I sometimes thought, to hold me apart from all the rest— seemed to say, "I may flirt with others and play with them, but not with *you*. We stand on different ground. We must be lovers—or nothing." I now believe Christina acted in this from a high deliberate motive; I do believe she thought the memory of our past too sacred to be profaned by any contact with the commonplace and frivolous flirtations in which it was sometimes her humour to indulge. Then I thought, according to my mood, that she was resolved to repel me utterly, or resolved to make me her slave; and I sometimes adored and sometimes hated her.

Perhaps I might have taken heart of grace
and broken loose altogether from her, and stood
up and been free, but for the expression with
which I sometimes—only sometimes—caught her
eye resting on mine. Old, sweet, sad memories
seemed to shine in it, and to bring our hearts
together for the moment once again. This happened more often when we were on the stage than
at any other time. Always the moment my eye
thus met hers she turned away, and her expression and manner changed; and when next I met
her she was sure to be colder than ever to me,
and perhaps to be more ostentatiously friendly
than ever to somebody else whom I especially
disliked. There were many whom I disliked on
her account, believing one week that she surely
cared about them, and finding out the week after
that she held them in the most absolute and
supreme indifference.

Thus, then, the season mooned away. Thus
it came about that, though I had succeeded, was
the tenor of the season, and at the best house;
sang with Christina Reichstein, helped towards

her success, and shared it; saw her frequently off the stage,—she received her friends at her lodgings in Jermyn-street on Sunday evenings, and one or two off afternoons in the week,—was a constant visitor, and perhaps ought to be very happy—I was distracted, disappointed, and miserable.

What, on earth, was the reason why I so hated to see Christina acting and singing with anybody but myself? What was it to me? Nevertheless I always felt keenly annoyed when the chances of the situation flung her literally into the arms of some stout basso, who probably felt no emotion whatever except anxiety about his own part, and its effect on the audience. She acted with such genuine and artistic effect, that I sometimes became ridiculously annoyed. She clasped her operatic fathers and lovers with a clasp apparently as fervent and impassioned as if they were genuine fathers or lovers, or only lay and feelingless figures. She never thought of them at the moment, as I knew well who had to embrace her publicly a dozen times a-week per-

haps, and knew how utterly absorbed in her lyrical art, and how absolutely indifferent to me, she
was all the time.

It would be idle to deny that stories of her
past life were whispered about which it was torture to hear, even though I knew that there was
no word of truth in them. I once got into a silly
row with a fellow who named the very year in
which he knew, he said, that she was living *au
cinquième* in a house in the Quartier Latin, with
a young artist whom she afterwards threw over,
and who accordingly took to absinthe, and finally
to the Montmartre Cemetery. The story-teller
fixed upon the very year before Christina's father
died, and when she was living peacefully and
working hard, poor girl, in our quiet old town by
the sea—before she had set foot on Paris pavement. I hardly ever indeed heard any story,
good or bad, told about her which my own personal and certain knowledge did not enable me
to contradict. One reason for this was, that so
far as her recent years — her years of growing
celebrity—were concerned, nobody had a word to

say against her. Her life had left no opening for
suspicion, or even for calumny. But a beautiful
and attractive woman in that line of life, who has
cruelly sinned by her sudden and signal success,
must have done wrong some time or other, you
know; and as there is nothing to be said against
her during the years which were passed under our
own observation and those of our associates, the
inference is obvious—the error must have been
committed in the obscurer years before we came
to know anything of her. Therefore three out of
every four of the stories whispered about her referred to those dear old early days when her life
surely was one of the calmest and purest that
even a German girl could live.

There was apparently some mystery about her
marriage. That she had been married appeared
to be certain : most people said she was a widow.
Ned Lambert did not know; he said he always
took it for granted that she had married the
Italian who had had her educated and brought
out, and that he had died, or they had separated
somehow. This was the only scrap of mystery

—if it was mystery—about her; and she lived
an open, frank, and fearless life, absolutely like
one who had nothing to conceal. A steady,
elderly German woman always lived with her; a
woman of some intelligence and education, with
a great eye for artistic make-up, and a good
business memory,—a sort of compound of poor
relation, paid companion, and lady's maid.

Christina never talked to anybody of her past
life, or indeed much of herself at all. She had
a great many friends, and was free, friendly, and
joyous with most of them.

I made slight allusions several times to the
old town of her early life and mine; but she did
not seem inclined to go back to any such memories, although she showed not the slightest em-
barrassment on the subject. Once, at last, when
I had again made allusion to it, she seated herself at the piano and sang, as her only answer—
I believe to an air of her own composition—a
little ill-humoured ballad by a German poetess,
whose name I now forget, expressing entire dis-
regard and contempt for all the associations of

the poetess's native town and early days, except
for the memory of an old tree which pleasantly
shaded her childhood. I ceased after that to say
any word which might remind her of that past
from which she had evidently made up her mind
to be wholly severed.

What I detested most was to see her haunted
by the presence of Mr. Lyndon, M.P. He was
always in attendance on her; and I hated him.
He ignored my existence when he could; I avoided
meeting him when I could. There was something about his manner to me which was always
strangely irritating; all the more so because there
was nothing in it on which a man could reasonably found any cause of offence. His bearing
ever seemed to say, " *You* are not a person to
be received by me as an equal. I know what
you were, and that is what I always choose
to think you. Others may regard you as a successful artist, and so, being like myself professed
patrons of art, may admit you to their intimacy.
I don't choose to see your success, or to care
about it. You may be tolerated by Madame

Reichstein; that is no reason why you should
be tolerated by me. I may make myself a slave
to her openly and ostentatiously; that is no
reason why I should be so condescending to *you*."
I am afraid there was something mean in my
dislike of him; my detestation of his cold arrogance, his insolent money-pride, his bearing even
among those of our artist-circle whom he specially
favoured. His very homage to Christina I thought
had something offensive in its ostentation. It
always seemed to say, " Behold what so great
and grand a personage as I can do for beauty
and art. I can come down from my serene respectability and be the cavalier in service of a
singing-woman."

Christina, however, did not seem to regard
his attentions in that light. She encouraged him,
flattered him, trifled with him, coquetted with
him; sometimes had long and serious talks with
him in the corners of crowded rooms. He took
her to the Ladies' Gallery to hear the debates
on nights when there was no opera. He hardly
ever spoke himself, or intended to do so; but

he was a steadfast Whig party-man ; and people
said ministers thought a great deal of him, and
that he might have been in office if he liked.
He was often on the platform—sometimes in the
chair—at Bible-society meetings and missionary
meetings; and he was dead against opening places
of amusement—or even the British Museum—
on Sundays. He had his vices, but they were
very quiet and decorous. His looks and his ways
with women—the women I usually saw him with
—had a cold, consuming sensuousness which I
thought detestable. He had been married twice,
and now had long been a widower; and he had
the repute of being the very best of fathers,
especially devoted to his youngest daughter, who
never thwarted him, as her rigidly religious sisters
did, on the score of his operas and his singers
and his liking for the ballet. I never could quite
understand how a man could be greatly devoted
to his daughter, and wholly unscrupulous as regarded her sex in general. But it seemed Mr.
Lyndon was so. People admired him for the
former peculiarity, and thought none the worse

of him for the latter. He was commonly set down as an excellent man, of great ability and influence; and most persons paid court to him accordingly.

He was, I discovered, a great patron of Revolution. Refugees from disturbed continental countries were constantly seeking him out and being taken up and patronised by him. Christina too seemed always interested in that sort of thing; and they evidently used to have semi-official conferences about it. Observing this, I of course began to detest and despise all continental refugees; to regard them as humbugs, like Mr. Lyndon, and to think oppressed nationalities nuisances and shams. I could not believe that Christina really cared much about such business; and for Mr. Lyndon I set it down at once that he had no other interest in it but that it ministered to his own consequence and importance. In fact, he was a patron, and only kind or even civil to those who approached him as such,—except of course women, who, when they were good-looking, carried claims of their own

about with them which commanded them to Mr.
Lyndon's attention. Moreover, he seemed to
take a sort of pleasure in watching the smallness
of human nature even in those he paid court to ;
and he laughed a short and sharp laugh over any
small humiliation to which his closest favourite
might happen to be put.

Thus the man presented himself to my observation. I never knew anything worse of him
than just what I have told or indicated; but I
strongly disliked him; and as, thank Heaven, I
never approached him as one approaches a patron,
or recognised his right of patronage, he never
was anything better than coldly civil to me—and
not even that when he could with decency avoid
it. If afterwards I may have pained or injured
the man, not quite without malice, I may at
least explain why it was that from the first and
to the last I detested and despised him.

Christina sometimes gave suppers at her
rooms (please to remember that I am describing
the ways of ten or a dozen years ago), and I
used to meet some of her sister-singers there,

and one or two military men, and a few of the leading critics, whom no actor or singer is ever indifferent about conciliating. I was generally found at these gatherings, chiefly because, although I hated to be there, I could not help myself, and had not the spirit to stay away. They seemed to me entirely frivolous, hollow, heartless. Christina herself appeared to have sunk quite down to the level of her surroundings. The conversation was for the most part mere gabble and gossip and satire. Everyone paid court to the ruling artists who happened to be present by sneering at their absent rivals. Hostile critics were denounced and no doubt calumniated. Stories were told of the presents made by such a tenor to such a critic to explain the tremendous puffs with which this or that journal, defying all audiences and musical science and common sense, flamed in the forehead of the morning sky. Counter - insinuations were made about the diamond-rings, and other temptations yet more bewitching, with which this or that soprano or contralto had vainly sought to corrupt the impreguable honour of another critic who happened to be one of the company.

The literary gentlemen did not appear to have much more *esprit de corps* than the singers. If the latter babbled all manner of hissing stories against their rivals, the former listened complacently and even assentingly to the keenest insinuations against the honour and the trustworthiness of brother critics. The critics seemed to have an enormous estimate of their own power; and not an unreasonable estimate, judging from the court paid to them by those who ought to be best able to appreciate their influence. No one seemed to think much about the public at all. It was quite a matter between the artists and the critics. If these approved of and wrote up those, the thing seemed to be done.

From my own point of view it did not thus appear to me. I had always relied on the audience rather than on the critics, and indeed had been somewhat ignored by the latter. I owe them no ill-will on that account. Frankly, they were right. Even then I had arrived at a very

fair estimate of my own merits. I knew that I
had a voice and nothing else. My soul was not
in the art; and I felt satisfied that some time or
other this must be found out by the public. I
was quite aware that I had not one ray of the
inspiration which lighted the soul and the eyes
of Christina Reichstein in some of her great
parts. I knew that I was little better than a
musical automaton; but I was a success with
the audiences for all that. The opera-house and
the concert-room filled for me; and had my voice
only endured I must have made a fortune. The
critics could not do much to serve me; and they
seemed rather too puzzled by my success to go
boldly in for attacking me.

One evening I remember in particular. Some
dozen or so supped at Christina's rooms. It so
happened that this night she took hardly any
notice of me, certainly distinguished me in no
way from the most commonplace of her ordinary
visitors. Mr. Lyndon sat at her right hand, and
paid her devoted and undisguised attention, which
she took with a quiet assent that half-maddened

me. On her left sat a distinguished critic and
littérateur, who had written successful plays and
successful novels, published capital translations
of various foreign works, edited scientific volumes,
compiled biographies, and even varied the more
laborious occupations of his life by appearing occasionally as an amateur actor. He had an astonishing power of conversation; he could talk
with marvellous fluency and vivacity on all subjects, and almost in all European languages. To
this gentleman Christina always intimated that
she owed a great deal. He had been, it would
appear, one of the first to note and to welcome
her success. He was too, as I afterwards heard
from her many a time, one of the few who understood that she was something more than a mere
singer. Indeed, the criticisms he had published
about her did show a deep and genuine apprecia-
tion of all those qualities of her voice, her lyrical
style, her dramatic power, which were most truly
great and peculiar. There was nothing in him
which was not apparently sincere and manly. It
did not even then surprise me that he had mani-

fested no particular admiration for *my* genius and merits. He had taken my success, such as it was, quietly, and as one whom nothing on the part of the public could astonish; and he had said nothing ill-natured, or satirical, or even distinctly depreciatory of me, only said just as little of me as might be—habitually recorded the fact that I won applause, and so let me go my way.

Ordinarily I should have felt little of anger towards anybody who, like myself, did not think me a great singer. But this particular night I felt altogether out of humour with myself, and naturally therefore inclined to be put easily out of humour with everybody else. I was beginning of late (for reasons to be more fully explained presently) to doubt myself, to suspect that I was capable of playing a mean and ignoble part, to look on myself as capable of servile love and low-minded rancour. I was beginning to be ashamed of my slavish hanging after Christina's skirts, and to feel abashed and perplexed by other weaknesses too. I thought I saw myself sinking, and that others must see it as well. So

I came prepared, despising myself, to resent any
slight from another.

I soon became exasperated when I saw that
to the critic I have spoken of, Madame Reichstein
ostentatiously paid special attention this night.
She flirted with him in the most fearless and determined manner ; it appeared to me, with some
definite purpose : whether for the discomfiture of
myself or Mr. Lyndon I could not determine.
The critic, who had flirted doubtless with all the
prima donnas of the previous ten years, entered
very vivaciously into the game, and of course
took it in precisely the spirit in which it was
started.   But I chose to be deeply offended ; and
the more deeply I felt, the more deeply I drank
for comfort and desperation.   I paid extravagant
attention to a little Frenchwoman (a new singer)
beside me, who was herself drinking champagne
with amazing zest.   I either saw, or thought I
saw, some smiles passing around at both of us,
and especially it seemed to me that a look of
surprise and contempt came up on the face of
Christina's pet critic.   Impelled by Heaven knows

what idiotic notion, I jumped on my feet and proceeded to address the astonished little company.
I complained that I had been insulted ; I poured
out some frantic nonsense, especially composed
of denunciations of critics and literary men.   I
saw Mr. Lyndon raise his double-eyeglass, survey
me coolly for a moment, and then drop his glass
and resume his conversation with his neighbour
as if nothing I could do ought to be surprising
or worth any particular notice.   Looks of anger,
contempt, pity, or disgust were on every face, and
one I could see even then wore an expression of
such surprise and shame and sorrow, that it
might almost have brought me back to my
senses.

I believe I displaced the mirth, broke the
good meeting.   But I really am not quite certain how the matter ended, except that I was
assisted to a cab by a brother artist and the
very critic I had been so absurdly denouncing.
And I have a pretty clear idea. as shame flashed
a gleam of consciousness over me, that I heard
the former say to the latter, "Never saw him

like this before, I'm sure; can't think what came over him. He is a very good fellow generally, I can assure you."

And the critic replied: "Yes; I have no doubt he is a good fellow, and he has an uncommonly fine voice; but what a confounded fool he must be!"

CHAPTER VI.

BITTERLY and severely did I echo next morning the opinion of my friend the critic. What a confounded fool I had made of myself! was the first thought present to my mind. How *she* must have despised me! How steadily I had been sinking of late! This proof, the most grotesque and ridiculous humiliation I had ever been put to, was perhaps not the sharpest proof of a lowered nature which pricked my conscience.

For I had yet a conscience and a sense of honour. I have read somewhere a story of a prince to whom a loving fairy gave a magical ring, which was to be his guide and guard through life. Whenever he did wrong, the ring was to prick his finger—sharply, in proportion to the magnitude of his fault. He erred and erred; was

pricked and pricked. At last he could not stand
the thing any longer; and so he angrily plucked
the ring off his finger and flung it away. For a
while he was perfectly happy, and could do as he
liked unpricked of conscience. But of course I
need not say that he went to the bad utterly—
unless, perhaps, the fairy came in and somehow
redeemed him in the end. Now I had not thrown
away my ring, and I felt its sharp pressure very
keenly even if I had not conscience and spirit
enough to do right and thus avoid its censure.

Two things, at all events, I must do. I must
make a humble apology to Christina, and another
to Mr. Levison, the critic. The latter gave me
no troubling thought; I knew he would receive it
like a gentleman, and, indeed, that he was not
likely in any case to feel much about the matter.
But to meet Madame Reichstein and talk of my
shame to her was something quite different—
something I dreaded. Perhaps I dreaded it none
the less because I saw how altered were our relations now; and I expected from her none of that
tender, forgiving interest with which women who

care for us as lovers, or brothers, or friends, are only too happy to anticipate our penitence and cover our humiliation.

It had to be done, however; and with an aching head and dogged heart I set about doing it. I lived now, since the Lyndons had left London, in the same house with Edward Lambert. We had taken lodgings together in Brompton; and though our hours and ways differed so much that I sometimes did not meet him for whole days together, we were still friendly as ever, with only one or two subjects on which we suspended, rather than withheld, reciprocal confidence. All this I shall presently come to; for the moment I pass it by.

This particular morning I was glad not to see him; I did not want to talk to anybody. I dressed myself as carefully and well as I could; but it seemed, as I nervously and often scrutinised my appearance, that I could not get a certain dissipated and rowdy look out of my eyes and hair. All that tubbing, and sponging, and brushes, and pomade, and perfumery could

do was done energetically; but I still thought
the rowdy look remained, like the blood-spots on
Lady Macbeth's hands or Bluebeard's key. My
soul sickened at the thought of breakfast. I re-
jected eggs and toast and kidneys, and would not
look at the *Times*. When something like a rea-
sonable hour had approached, I started on my
errand, and walked to Jermyn-street.

When I stood at the door, this soft and sunny
noon, I could not but think of the drear and
dripping night when, prouder of soul and purer
of heart than now, I stood at this same door and
sought Christina in vain. Since then I had many
times crossed the threshold, but never sought to
speak with her alone and face to face. If we were
to speak together now, in a room alone, it would
be for the first time since the night when she
called a farewell to me, and the rose dropped from
her bosom.

I sent up my card, was invited to come up,
and I found her alone.

The room was small, elegant, with nothing
even in the graceful carelessness of its appearance

to remind one of the profession. Everything was quiet, unpretentious, and even homely - looking. Christina had been playing on the piano and singing in a low tone as I came; and when I entered the room she had just turned round and was rising to meet me. She was dressed in a morning-robe of purple cashmere, or some such material, with a white rose in her bosom. The colour of the dress made her bright complexion, luxuriant fair hair, and deep dark eyes look even more striking and dazzling than they were wont to do, and her hair now fell around her as unconfined and careless as when it used to rouse the spinster-like anger of good Miss Griffin in the choir long ago. Rising from the piano she threw back her hair with one hand and with an impatient toss of the head, and then held out her other hand to me. She scarcely looked up, and our eyes did not meet.

"You see," she said with a smile, "how entirely without ceremony I receive you. My hair is in terrible disarray; but if you will make such early morning calls, what can one do?"

"I ought to apologise to you for coming, and

I would do so if I had not so much more serious an apology to make. I am ashamed of myself, Madame Reichstein, and of the world; and, most of all, of *you*."

"What an alarming preface! What have you done?"

"It is useless kindness, Madame Reichstein, to profess ignorance. You know only too well what I have done to shame myself, and what I have come to apologise for. Don't, Christina—don't force me to think you have really lost all interest in me by telling me that you were not angry with me, or ashamed of me, for what happened last night."

I had till now been standing, and Christina had not left her music-stool. While I was speaking, she rose, and came towards me.

"Emanuel," she said gravely, "I am glad to hear you speak in this way. I am glad indeed; and I will not go on in the tone I tried to take. I *was* angry with you for—for what happened last night. I was angry, and deeply pained, and ashamed—on your account. I could not recognise you last night; but I am glad to believe you could not recognise yourself, and my mind is much relieved. I have thought of it ever since; but now, if you bid me, I will think of it no more. You are not changed, Emanuel? Not really changed, I mean? You have not allowed the world to corrupt you? There was a word or two which used to be favourite with you once—about keeping the whiteness of the soul. You have kept the whiteness of your soul, *nicht wahr?*"

She spoke with a friendly confiding tenderness and frankness, as unlike her ordinary manner now as my drunken display of the previous night could be to my penitent sadness of this morning.

" I hope I have not changed wholly, Christina. I hope so. But times have changed, and most people round me; and I sometimes think and fear that I have been allowing myself to sink into something of which once I should have been ashamed."

She laid her hand gently on mine.

" Emanuel, I too fear it. I have watched you closely—from friendship, believe me; and I do fear that you are allowing yourself to—well, not to improve."

" Can you wonder at it ?" I interrupted her in bitter tone. " What have I to care for? Why should I care for myself? If I have changed, have not you changed? Are you the same that you were? Do I not see that you can fling yourself into a frivolous and foolish life ?"

" Do you want answers to all these questions, Emanuel ?"

" No, I don't; I have no right to ask them. I have nothing to do with your way of living, or your friends, or the people you allow to hang after you, or the reports that other people spread about—I want no answer, Christina; but when you reproach me with having changed, and sunk, and all that, I can only—"

" Tell me to look at myself, Emanuel, and bring my moral lessons to bear *there*, you were going to say."

" No, I was not going to say that, although— But I was not going to say it, indeed. I was only going to say that I never set up for anything, for great moral purpose, or nobleness, or virtue, or any of that sort of thing. I take my colour—most men do—from the hues of those around them. You, Christina, were my dream for long, long years; and you know it. Well, I am awake; and I can't pretend to be dreaming any more. We are all poor creatures, I suppose; and I accept the situation, and don't set up to be any better than my neighbours. I am heartily ashamed of what I said and did last night, and I apologise profoundly for it. I offended you, and insulted your guests, and made a beast and a brute of myself; and it is very kind of you to receive me at all after such a scandal. But for the rest I have not much to say. I have not improved of late; and that's all."

I could not keep back the bitterness of my soul; it found relief, and I was not sorry. Christina did not wince, however; no, not in the least.

"Emanuel, *zwischen uns sei Wahrheit*. You remember the old scene in *Iphigenia?* Between us be the truth! You think I have greatly changed, and for the worse?"

I made no answer.

"Come, speak out," she said impatiently. "You think I have become worldly and frivolous and cunning, don't you?"

"Sometimes I do, Christina."

"I asked you when we met for the first time —I mean the first time since long ago—not to judge me merely from the outside. I don't show to advantage—and I don't always want to; but I don't wish to lose your good opinion wholly, Emanuel; the more as you seem to make my falling-off a sort of excuse for your own. Come," she said, and she sat in a chair and pointed me to another—"come and tell me my faults. Be a friend, and speak out. I have spoken frankly to you."

"To-day, just for this moment, you have."

"To-morrow, perhaps, I shall be cold and careless and frivolous; very likely I shall seem so. *You*, I might have thought, could judge a little better than by mere seemings. Well, will you tell me my faults?"

"No; and I have not been speaking of faults;

only of the change that seems to have come over you."

"Then I will speak for you. You think I have no heart and no memory, and no care for anything but flattery and excitement?"

"I have lately thought so."

"Then you are wrong, Emanuel; indeed, indeed you are. I have a sort of part to play, and I must play it. I do not deny that I love praise and excitement; but I could have loved other things better; and I still am no more in heart what you commonly see me than I am Amina or Leonora."

"Why do you keep that old man hanging after you?"

"I might reply by another question, and say, What right have you to ask? I might evade the question for a moment, as most women would, I think, and innocently ask, What old man? But I suppose of course you mean Mr. Lyndon. Well, Mr. Lyndon has long been an intimate friend of mine, and—"

"And is likely soon to be more, people say."

"Do they?   How kind people are!   What do they say?"

"Well, five out of every six say you will marry him."

She smiled.

"Indeed!   And the sixth—who I suppose has reason to know better—what does he say on the subject?"

"Even he, I think, knows no particular reason to the contrary."

"Do *you* know no reason to the contrary?"

"None whatever."

"Then you know nothing of my life for the past few years?"

"Nothing.   Except, of course, what all the world knows."

She sighed audibly.

"I am glad of it," she said;   "you shall know it all some time—before long, perhaps, but not now.   For a while, Emanuel, take me on trust; I am better than I seem.   Listen, and I will speak to you as I never meant to speak to you again. Your good opinion is dear to me.   Your friend-

ship I would have, if I could.   Once, Emanuel, I
loved you better than all things on earth, except
—see how frank I am !—except success."

I could not repress a groan ; and I rose from
my chair and turned partly away.

"But I always dreamed of that success with
you.   And you loved me ; but not so deeply and
wholly—no, don't speak ; if I am stayed now I
shall never be able to continue—not so deeply as
I would have had.   We went our ways, hoping to
meet again before it should be too late.   We did
not so meet ; it was too late.   When I wrote to
you in London, Emanuel, it was too late."

"No, no, Christina ; no, by Heaven !   It was
the idlest chance, the purest delusion, the error of
of a kindly, well-meaning friend that made you
think—"

"All that I have since learned, or guessed.
But I did not and could not know it then ; and
you kept yourself hidden away until I hated you
and myself for the unwomanly advance I had
made, and the silence that followed it."

"I never knew, I never dreamed, that Mdlle.

Reichstein was Christina Braun; and I was poor and obscure and hopeless, a beggar without a name."

"Well, it is vain talking; let all that be laid aside. It is now too late, and Providence has kindly ordered it for the best. I have only brought back all this that I may say one thing for myself. I have chosen another part in life, and I mean to play it faithfully and loyally to the end. Therefore, Emanuel, I have kept back from you, and received you not even as a friend. If we were friends, you might come to know in time why I do things which appear to you now strange. I cannot have you think badly of me. Your word, Emanuel; can we be friends?"

She held her hand out frankly, and her eyes met mine.

"You do not speak. Will you be my friend? Your word, and I shall expect that, once pledged, it shall be as your oath. Will you be my friend?"

I could not answer for a moment; I could not answer unconditionally at all. For half a life I had loved her; lately I had almost hated her. How could I in a moment promise to subside into pure and enduring friendship? I saw that in her eyes there came a look of anxiety and pity and pathos. She leaned now on the chimneypiece and looked steadfastly at me.

"Christina," I answered at last, and in tones that only struggled to be calm and clear, "I will do my best; I will indeed. That is my promise."

She held her hand out again, and I raised it and touched it with my lips. I noticed that it was the left hand, and I saw the plain hoop of gold on the third finger.

Her eyes too fell upon it; and she coloured and looked embarrassed. She glanced at me doubtingly, inquiringly, as one who considers whether the time has not come to make some confession.

I wish I had allowed her or encouraged her to speak; but I did not. I had little doubt that there was some painful story — I would not call it secret—connected with her past life;

either that she had lost by death a husband whom she loved, or had been separated from one who was not worthy of her. In either case I shrank with keen sensitiveness from provoking a confidence which must be painful. Despite my pledge of friendship just made, I could not speak to Christina of her husband. I rose to take my leave.

"We understand each other, Emanuel, again, do we not?" she asked hesitatingly.

"Better at least than before, Christina."

"And you will not, I hope and pray, throw away your time and your prospects on—on folly and people unworthy of you."

"Some kind friend, Christina, has evidently been telling good-natured tales of me."

"No; but I have heard, and I have even myself observed, things that grieved me."

"Well, Christina, I mean to reform. I hope to become a model member of society; almost, perhaps, like your friend Mr. Lyndon."

"You talk lightly and bitterly. It pains me to hear you."

"Forgive me; I will not talk lightly or bitterly if I can. I do mean to improve. I am not nearly so bad, Christina, as some of my friends or yours appear to think. But I am ashamed of myself; and I will try to take up again the broken threads of my life. I confess that I find life sometimes rather bitter and barren; and I don't well know what particular gain one has from living and struggling at all."

"Nor I, Emanuel, sometimes. But we still live, my dear; and we must do our best to make life worth having. Do you think life is more of a restraint and a disappointment to you than to me? Do you think you have less to hope for or more to strive against in every way than I have? Are you the only one who has to crush-down warm and dear feelings? Ah, no, Emanuel! There are others who are more tried, and have less chance of escaping. Hush!—don't speak; did you hear nothing?"

She went to the window and looked out. It opened casement-fashion, and I saw that she was about to throw it open and apparently to step out on the little balcony in front; but she checked herself, and after a mere glance into the street, drew cautiously back. Her face was very pale when she turned to me, and her eyes shone with a lustre the more striking.

I was about to speak, but she raised her hand to enjoin silence. I remained silent, and without moving. The street outside was singularly quiet. It seemed as if sleeping in the hot glare of the sun. From where I stood I could see through the window only a part of the far side of the street. There was no life stirring there; not even a hurdygurdy was heard. For the few seconds we remained silent not a cab rattled down the street. In the room nothing was heard but the ticking of the little gilt clock on the chimneypiece. When, as we stood and looked at each other, a piano-string suddenly snapped, the clang came so loud and sharp on the ear that Christina positively started.

Then, in the silence which followed, I heard— just what I had heard before in fact, as Christina broke off our conversation—three bars of what seemed to be an operatic air, but which was certainly unfamiliar to me, whistled in the street below. The whistle was of a somewhat peculiar kind, shrill and sibilating; and the whistler stopped suddenly short at one particular note each time; almost as a bird does which is trying to learn some air from its master, and cannot get over some difficult turn, and so stops and begins again. I marked all this now because my ears and senses were on the stretch for something; otherwise I should never have paid any attention to it, or perhaps even been aware of the sound at all. It was, however, the only sound to be heard; and it was clear that Christina was listening to it with all her ears.

Her face, from paleness, had grown to a deep flush of excitement, and her lips quivered visibly. When the whistling had the second time reached the same note, she sighed audibly, as with profound resignation or profound relief, one could not tell which.

"Has anything happened?" I asked.

"O yes; something has happened. Something very unexpected. I must ask you to leave me, Emanuel."

"Two words only. Nothing bad?"

"No; something good, very good. I did not expect it yet. I ought to be deeply thankful; I am thankful. Good-morning, Emanuel. Please don't ask me any more; and don't stay."

She was all trembling, and quite eager and excited.

I obeyed her and put no further questions, but hurried from the room. Just as I was leaving, her German companion or follower came in, looking excited too, but seemingly in a wholly joyous sense. She came like one who brings good news.

When I reached the street, I could see nobody on either side of it who seemed likely to have been the mysterious whistler. A man was wheeling a barrowful of fruit, wrapped in blue papers, along towards the St. James's-street end. A policeman was tramping the other way. A girl, with a roll of music in her hand, and petticoats high kilted, passed close to me. Other human beings near at hand I could not see. It did not seem likely that any one of those I had seen could have had the faculty of startling Christina by whistling the fag-end of a tune.

CHAPTER VII.

THE conversation I had just had with Christina
will help still further to explain a little of my
past life. It was certain that I had degenerated
since the renewal of our acquaintanceship. Life
has to be got through somehow after the heaviest
disappointment; and not often in real existence
can we raise a Rolandseck over the wasted scene
of frustrated love and ruined hope, and go and be
pious and patient there. It was only after I had
met Christina again that the full bitterness of the
thought came to me that I had no longer anything to live for. While we were separated there
was always an object, if not a hope. Now there
seemed neither. I confess that I sank a little
way into a sort of unmeaning joyless dissipation,
for which I had naturally no taste, and into which

I could not by any possibility throw my soul. The champagne of the night and the headache of the morning just a little distracted me, and no more. Ned Lambert sometimes shook his honest head and tried a gentle laconic remonstrance; with the usual effect. I have no doubt he spoke to Christina on the subject, and urged her to bring her influence to bear. Perhaps to this I owed the pledge of friendship we had just made.

Anyhow, the pledge of friendship did not procure me much more of Christina's society, or apparently of her confidence. There was perhaps a warmer pressure of the hand when we met; and there was occasionally a deeper shade of interest and anxiety in her eyes as they rested on me for a moment. Sometimes I fear I only set this down to her dread on the score of my degenerating habits; and I felt rather inclined to resent than to feel grateful for it.

No explanation had come or suggested itself regarding her sudden emotion on the day when our ceremonial of friendship - vowing was so strangely interrupted.

Mr. Lyndon of course often came to the Opera. One night, just about this time, I observed him enter the stalls rather late. He came in along with a tall, thin, dark-bearded, remarkable-looking man—a man with a high forehead, sloping rather back and seamed with premature wrinkles; a man with a face which would have been stern and sharp in its expression but for a certain soft and melancholy sweetness in his liquid luminous eyes. There was something about this man's appearance which attracted me in an instant; and I could not help thinking it attracted Christina too, for I observed that from time to time she glanced under her eyes in the direction where he and Lyndon sat; and she was too much of a true artist ever to think under ordinary conditions of sending her eyes roaming about the house in search of admiration. If you could have got a boxful of emperors, Christina Reichstein would have scorned to sing at them. So I had some reason for silent surprise when I observed that she did now and then glance quietly in the direction where this man was sitting with his friend. He was, I perceived, usually very marked and emphatic in his applause.

Mr. Lyndon and this man escorted Christina to her little brougham after the opera. Needless to say that I did not feel much inclined to obtrude myself on such company. Christina saw me, and called a friendly good-night, with two or three words added in German, which bade me see her as early as possible next day. Mr. Lyndon and I exchanged, as usual, a very cold salute.

As I turned away I met a brother artist, whom I saw exchanging a salute a little more friendly with the dark and pale-faced stranger.

"Who's our friend?" I asked, nodding in the direction of the stranger, who had gone with Mr. Lyndon to the carriage of the latter. I threw an immense amount of scorn into my voice; why, I don't know. He to whom I spoke was a Frenchman.

"But I have forgot his name. He is an Italian, —indeed, that goes without saying,—and he is going to be a lion of your salons here for a season, I am told. He is a patriot; he is an escaped—"

" Convict ?"

" Convict—yes; that is, Austrian convict, or at least, Austrian prisoner."

" I thought he had a look of Toulon about him."

"Nothing of the sort. You are not *sympathique;* nor I indeed, no more. He has escaped somehow from Spielberg, or death, or something, and he is going to agitate your country to take up arms for the independence of Italy. And she will! O yes; England will spend all her moneys, and her powders and shots, and her cottons, just for a dream."

" But this person ?"

" Well, that is all I know. He is a very distinguished man—quite celebrated."

" Whose name you have forgotten."

" Yes, and of whom I never heard before."

" How did you come to know him ?"

" Madame Reichstein did me the honour to present me."

" How does *she* know him ?"

" O, for that, my dear, you must not ask

me. Perhaps your Lyndon has taken him in charge."

"Ah, very likely; he patronises illustrious foreigners a good deal."

"But rather when they are in *jupons* than in pantaloons, is it not? Where are you going?"

"Home, I think."

"Ridiculous—at this hour? Come and have a game of billiards."

"Thanks—not to-night."

"Come at least and smoke a pipe."

"No; I can't to-night."

Indeed my pipe was quite put out for that evening. I cannot tell how it was that I came to associate the man I had seen in the stalls with the scene in Christina's room the other day; but I did so associate him in my mind at once. When, as she was leaving the theatre, she asked me to come and see her next day,—asked me in pressing tones, and in German (we hardly ever spoke German to each other now),—I felt in some strange way my conjecture was confirmed. I went home moodily, expecting something painful, I hardly knew what.

Christina received me very graciously when I visited her next morning—very graciously and sweetly. There was a pathetic, anxious sort of kindness about her manner which was not usual with her of late. She was embarrassed too, and her thoughts seemed dwelling on anything rather than the subject we first talked of. For a few minutes there was indeed an awkward pause every now and then in the conversation we carried on, as if each was expecting the other to put some question or begin some explanation.

We spoke a few words about Ned Lambert and his love, and his separation from Lilla Lyndon, of which Christina appeared to know a good deal. I made some allusion to the one great cause of Lilla's resolution to leave London, and found that Christina seemed to understand or have guessed it.

" That, too, I know," she said. " You speak of the wretched man, Stephen Lyndon ?"

" I do."

" I did not know his real name or his real nature until lately." (Here she paused.) " But I don't want to speak of him just now. I have

sent for you for another purpose, Emanuel." Another pause—and then she said: "I am going
to introduce you to-day to a man whose friend I
want you to be; for my sake first, and then for
his own. I wish you and him to be friends, and
I wish that you should know our secrets. You
saw me speak to a tall and dark-haired Italian
last night?"

"I did."

"He will come here to-day. He is my husband."

Christina dropped her eyes as she spoke the
words, and I was glad that no gaze was on me;
for, despite all that had come and gone, this was
a heavy shock. Spoken suddenly, firmly, the
words seemed to go through me like a rifle-bullet
or the thrust of a sword.

Then she looked up again, and a faint sweet
smile came over her face, and our eyes met
frankly; and she held out her hand to me across
the table, as if in obedience to some involuntary
and kindly impulse.

I pressed it silently. Thus we sealed our new

friendship, and the dream of my boyhood was really over.

After a moment's pause she said : " My husband is an Italian, as you see. His name is Carlo Farini Salaris. He had a title and orders and honours ; but he dropped them all because he was disappointed in Charles Albert, and in others too. He had two passions in his life—music and his country. Chance brought him to know me when I was a poor girl,—an adventuress, many people would have called me,—a beggar almost. He liked my voice ; he had faith in me ; he had me educated ; he brought me out. All that I am he made me. All that I could do for him in return I have done, I am doing."

" I knew that—that you had been married, Christina. I did not know that your husband was living."

" Nor must you know it now. Understand me, it is a secret only known to you, and perhaps one or two others. He has only lately escaped from an Austrian prison, where he was sent for the part he took in Lombard plots and revolu-

tions. He has escaped only, I fear, to take part
in other plots. Think how happy the life of his
wife must be! I can help him, however, in many
ways while I am not known to be his wife. I
have carried the fiery cross for him from the Alps
to the Straits of Messina, when not even Austrian
or Neapolitan police suspected the German soprano of being an emissary of the revolution. Ah,
it would be a long and weary tale to tell; it is a
sad memory! In this way I hold my life at his
disposal, and my happiness. I will plot for him,
scheme for him; smile while I know that he is
in danger, flirt when every moment I think to
hear news of his death. This is the only way in
which I can repay him : I owe him all."

"Surely you have given him something that
might repay anything he has done for you?"

"I have given him all I could, Emanuel; and
he was generous enough to have confidence in
me, and to believe that I would have given him
more if I could. Listen, and I will speak to you
with a frankness which others might misunderstand, but you will not. I will speak to you as if

I were a ghost come back from the grave, to whom the world could no longer have reality, and who had nothing more to do with human hopes, and loves, and misunderstandings, and all the rest of it. Even before I had made a success of any kind, he would have married me, and I would not. You know the reason why. I succeeded through him altogether. He pressed me again and again—tenderly, delicately, like a man with a noble nature. I was coming to England. For the first time since I had left it, you understand. He guessed why I was coming, and I told him all."

"All? All of the past, or—"

"I spoke to him as freely as some of his own countrywomen do to their confessor. I told him that I loved you—yes, I am not ashamed to say it now, and I was not then—and that my dearest hope was to find you. And he said, with his melancholy smile, 'Go to England; but if you do not find him, or have any cause to change your purpose, then promise me that you will come back to me.' I went to England, and you know the rest—Fate was against us."

"Fate was cruelly against *me!*" I said, start-
ing up; "Fate was against *me!* And you too,
Christina! You threw me away at a word; you
had done so before. Don't tell me of love—you
never loved me; you were too glad to escape from
me; you had your ambition and your career, and
you followed your destiny. Well, I don't blame
you, and I am not surprised. Peace be between
us for the future, and let us be friends if you
will; only do not torture me to no purpose by
trying to persuade me that that might have been
which never could have been. Well, forgive me
for interrupting you—"

"You have not interrupted me; the story is
all over. It was not very long to tell."

"O no; let me finish it. You saw me; and
I was poor and obscure; and you found no difficulty in taking the chance word of a good-natured,
thoughtless girl as decisive of my fate; and you
hurried back, and married your friend and patron,
who had influence and power. You were grateful
to him—quite right; and he exacted his recom-
pense for what he had done, and you gave him

yourself as his reward. Well, I offer you my con-
gratulations, and to him too. I am late in the
expression of my good wishes, but you must remember how well you kept the secret of your happiness, and that I thought you were a widow, not
a wife."

I saw Christina's cheek flush, and her eyes
first sparkle and then fill with tears; but I was
not in a mood to be stayed. Everything seemed
to have conspired to make me savage, and some
infernal spirit within appeared to drive me on,
adding word to word.

"Emanuel!"

"Yes; I thought you were a widow. So, I
suppose, did your other friend and patron, Mr.
Lyndon. *He* surely is not in your secrets? Or,
is he supposed to be your husband's friend, appointed to console you, and give you courage in
his absence and his dangers?"

"I have at least had no reason, as yet, to
repent of any confidence I may have placed in
him, as I have now to repent of the confidence
I placed in you. Emanuel, I know you will be

ashamed of your bitterness and your cruelty, and I forgive you beforehand. I know you have reason to complain. I owe you something, too; let me pay a part of my obligation by bearing patiently any insult you may choose to offer. You do not know how cruel you are. I have striven to be a devoted and loyal wife to my husband, as a brave German woman ought to be; and I have suffered much; and if I have had my ambition, it has not been fed for nothing, or bought without heavy penalty; and of the old days nothing remains; and now you insult and scorn me. It is much; but I bear it for the sake of old memories."

She had been seated on a sofa. She now stood up and leaned against the chimneypiece, and tossed her bright mass of hair back over her shoulders with the old familiar impatient action of one whom the weight of it oppressed in a moment of excitement. She looked so like the Christina of old that my anger melted away, and I bitterly repented my hasty words.

"I am always asking you to forgive me,

Christina; I must ask you now again, sincerely and humbly, for pardon. I was very bitter, and rude, and brutal, and I knew how unjust I was even at the time. But I only ask you to make some allowance for me. You know how I loved you. O, I am speaking now only of the past, and I might say it if your husband stood there ! I loved you deeply. No woman can be loved so twice in a life."

"I know it, Emanuel, and I do forgive you, freely and fully, your harsh words. You too must make allowance for me. My life is an anxious one in many ways. So far, it has been a failure ; and yet the best has passed. When I look at you, Emanuel, and make you my own mirror, I see that I too am no longer young. What a handsome fair-haired boy you were when I first saw you ! How many years ago ?"

" Twelve years ago."

" How old are you now ? You may tell me, I shall not betray confidence."

" I don't know—thirty-two or three."

" *Ach Gott!*—so old ! And I am—but that does not concern you to know. Yes, youth is gone for both of us. I am talking wildly to-day, am I not? Yes, I can't help it; but I don't often get into these moods. Youth is gone."

She turned to the mirror over the chimney-piece, and still keeping back her hair, gazed intently into her own face. Truth to speak, with all its lustrous beauty, there were faint, faint marks under the eyes, which hinted mournfully of Time's premature footprints.

"I was handsome, Emanuel, when a girl—was I not?"

She spoke without turning to me.

"You were beautiful; but surely you must know that you are still"—I was going to say, "that you are still beautiful;" but the expression of her face was so entirely abstracted and *distraite*, that the compliment, if it could be called one, died upon my lips.

"Yes," she went on, almost as one who talks in a dream, "I was very handsome, and very, very ambitious. I thought I was born for something great—born, perhaps, to conquer the world. You could not know how ambitious I was, and

how my heart was set on success; and nothing
has come of it after all."

"Nothing! and you the most successful of
the day?"

"Yes, the most successful of the day; but
who will be the most successful of to-morrow?
I shall sing perhaps another season or two, and
then be forgotten. I know well enough that I
am not like Giulia Grisi. *There* is a singer to
be remembered. I shall be extinguished when
I cease to sing. My success will die with the
echo of my voice. I have often thought that
I am like the man in my much-loved Schiller's
play, who says he staked his happiness and his
heaven on being a hero, and in the end no hero
was there, only a failure."

She leaned now on the chimneypiece, and
still contemplated her own face. I daresay an
ordinary looker-on would have thought there was
something theatric and self-conscious in her atti-
tudes and her ways. I did not think there was.
From her childhood almost—she was little more
than a child when first I knew her—there was

that rare and striking harmony of mind and body in her which made every word find unconsciously its natural expression in some gesture or attitude. This was not surely, one would have thought, a German attribute. Still less was it a faculty anyone can get up, or even cultivate. It came by nature. It made her a successful actress; it made her seem natural on the stage, because every action expressed so easily and gracefully the emotion which suggested it; it made her seem theatric off the stage, because so few people either will or can allow their moods to find any outward expression beyond that of voice and complexion.

She suddenly turned to me, and going back to the earlier part of our conversation, she said,

" You think I kept all this purposely a secret from you?"

I knew of course she meant her marriage and its story.

" I did think so, Christina."

" Well, perhaps it was partly a secret—at least, until I could learn what sort of person time and change had made *you*. Perhaps you did not at first show yourself in a manner which greatly invited confidence. Perhaps I fancied that you already knew nearly all the truth. Perhaps I may have thought—" and she stopped and sighed, and then smiled a strange, nervous, painful smile I did not like to see. Then she made a quick gesture with both hands as if she flung the subject from her, and came back to her seat. Looking at her watch, she said,

" My husband will be here soon. You know now why I was so much confused and embarrassed the last day you were here?"

" Yes; that was his signal I heard?"

" It was. He always whistles those few bars —first once, then again with the slight variation ; and I know he is coming. That is, you understand, when I have not seen him for some time— when his coming is unexpected; and it may be necessary to make some preparation to get rid of inconvenient visitors—"

" Like me ?"

" Like you that last day, before he knew you

or had given me leave to trust you. O, I am
thoroughly disciplined and obedient to him, believe me. I have heard that whistle in many
places—in places where I knew that a mistake
or a delay, or a precipitate motion on my part,
might involve his discovery and his death. I did
not expect to hear it so soon, although I knew
that the plan for his escape out of the Lombard
prison was in good hands and progressing well.
I have not a genius for conspiracy, Emanuel, and
they don't trust me much with details; even *he*
does not. I wait and watch and keep the secrets,
and do faithfully as I am told. And I have de-
nationalised myself for his sake, and forgotten my
country; indeed, had I not forgotten it long ago?
and I have learned to hope that the German sol-
diers may one day be chased across the Alps. My
husband is a man to inspire anyone with his own
hopes and his own will, as you are sure to discover
before long."

A card was put into Christina's hand, and
she directed that the visitor should be shown
up.

"It is *he*," she whispered to me when the servant had left the room. "*Here*, just now, he is only on my ordinary visiting-list. He is to me an Italian patriot who honours me with his acquaintance—no more."

In a moment Signor Salaris entered.

I do not know whether he had expected to find her alone, but in the mere flash of time from his announcement to his reaching Christina, I saw three distinct changes of expression in his face. His wife stood at one side of the chimney-piece, nearly opposite the door; I had fallen back to one of the windows looking into Jermyn-street. As he came in, I could see him, but he, naturally looking directly before him, did not see me. He crossed the threshold, therefore, with the formal bow of an ordinary visitor, and the corresponding expression. Apparently then, as he only saw his wife, he assumed that she was alone, and his pale face lighted up with a warm and bright expression, and he seemed for the instant, the second, like one rejoicing to throw off a weary disguise. And then he saw me; and with a change quick as the motion of light itself, his countenance subsided into the genial, courteous expression of one who presents himself to a friend. Probably no unprepared eye could have noted these changes. I saw them clearly, and they were significant of a character and a life.

Christina reassured him with a smile and a few words.

"My dear Carlo, here we are all friends, and you are my husband, not my visitor."

"Then this gentleman," he said, turning to me and speaking in excellent English, though a little slow and with a deep Italian accent, "this is Mr. Temple? I might have known him, indeed.—I have seen and heard you more than once, Mr. Temple, but I did not at first recognise you. I offer you my hand; I am, if you will allow me, your friend."

I gave him my hand, and we exchanged a cordial grasp. I think both our faces flushed. I felt mine grow hot. I know that across his pale cheek something faintly approaching to a crimson tinge came flashing, and a strange sud-

den spasm passed over it.   Can we be friends?
Here is the man who has robbed me of Christina; can I be his friend, sincerely, truly ?

I think so; at least I will try.   I like the expression of his face; I like his soft dark liquid
eyes, with an expression at once wild and gentle
and beseeching in them, like the eyes of a gazelle;
I like the contrast they present to the rigid, deep-
thinking, inflexible expression of the brow and
the lips and the chin.   I feel sure this man
has an unconquerable will, and a pure tender
heart.   He is artist and conspirator in one.   He
ought to have lived centuries ago, and been a
minstrel and a patriot at once.   Or he ought to
have lived half a century back or thereabouts, and
been a Girondist and led the chorus of the Mar-
seillaise on the day when he and his brothers went
out to die.

Yes, I liked the man at once; and as I looked
from his face to Christina's and noted her expression, I liked him all the better, for I felt an
indescribable pang of sympathy and pity for him.
His liquid loving eye looked melancholy when

it turned on her, and hers sank beneath his glance.

We talked like friends. He told me of his escape from prison in a pleasant simple kind of way, very agreeable, and even fascinating, to hear. There was a quiet modesty about all he said relating to himself that won upon one immensely. We talked of music and art, on which he was almost eloquent. When for a moment the conversation lapsed into what may be called generalities and conventional talk, he subsided into silence, and his mind evidently withdrew itself altogether into its own habitual thoughts.

I noted that Christina's eye always quietly followed his expressions of feature; I noted that the moment he lapsed into silence she changed the conversation, appealed directly to him with some question or other, and drew him forward again. I think I read their story.

"She has given herself to him," I thought, "and she esteems him, and fears *for* him; and she would love him if she could. But she cannot, and she knows it; and neither is happy. I read in his face high aim, and courage, and absolute self-devotion, and brooding perseverance—and failure. Whatever his hopes, they are doomed to fail."

Heavy and blank was the first feeling of disappointment with which I left Christina's house that day, knowing as a certainty and for the first time that she had a living, loving husband. But was I only disappointed—was the disappointment utter and without shade? Was there not some vague perception of a sense of relief? Month after month, year after year, I had worn myself out with almost unendurable agony of longing and disappointment, hopes and sickening pangs of despair; and now at last the doubt and the conflict of feeling were over, and I was released from the struggle. Now the torment of hope was quelled; now the worst was known; now the bitterness of death was past. Many a man sleeps, says the gaoler in Scott's romance, the night before he is executed, but no man the night before he is tried.

Yes, I felt a sense of relief. I should torture

myself with doubt and hope no more. I should walk up and down my room of nights trying to squeeze hope out of every word she had uttered, every glance I had caught—as shipwrecked sailors becalmed on a burning southern sea strive to squeeze moisture out of rags—no more. I should rehearse what I could say when next we met, or lament that I had not said this and that when last we met, no more. I should now be able to drudge through my life unvexed because hopeless.

A resolve, too, came up at once with a great new pang of relief. I had become a singer and taken to the lyric stage to please her, to win her, to prove to her that I could succeed; now I would give it up. I would cease to sham an artist's part, for which I really had no true taste or soul. I would go to some other country, to America, and see my brother. How fraternal we all grow, how we think of far-off brothers and sisters and mothers, when some woman has thrown us over! We are all like the gamester in the famous classic comedy of France, who

only remembers her to whom he owes his duty
when the luck of the night has gone against him.
I might have lived long enough content with very
rare and passing scraps of news from my brother,
but now a sudden and surprising tenderness
sprang up in my heart, and I wondered how I
had existed so long without seeing him; and I
quite resolved to go out to the States, and perhaps, with such money as I could get together,
join him in some new Western settlement, and
be a farmer. I thought of my own stout and
sinewy arms and rather athletic frame, and came
to the conclusion that, after all, digging, or fell-
ing trees, or hunting, was the sort of thing for
which Nature had clearly intended me.

In a word, I was used up, and wanted a new
and freshening life. I envied my Italian friend
his schemes and his aspirations, and thought I
should dearly like to have an oppressed nation-
ality to plot for, and if needs were, die for; and
I really wished I could, even through his influence,
get up within myself a sort of bastard philo-
Italianism, and fling myself into the cause of

Italy as so many Englishmen were beginning to do even then, and as Byron and Stanhope, and Hastings and Finlay, and so many others, had done for Greece. But I was never much of a politician; and I was so sick of the stage that I recoiled from the notion of converting my individual life into a new piece of acting. I had long come to think, and I do still think it seriously and profoundly, that nothing in life— no, nothing whatever—is so enviable as the capacity to merge one's individuality and very existence wholly in some great cause, and to heed no personal sacrifice which is offered in its name.

I don't much care whether the cause be political, or artistic, or scientific, or what not; let there but be a cause to which the individual is subjected, in which he freely loses himself, and I hold that man happy, if man can ever be happy at all. Never had it been my fortunate fate to have found such an object. My own profession never gave it to me. Therefore I accounted existence so far a failure. I had tried many modes of activity and amusement, and distraction and enjoyment, and they had done nothing for me, because I had never gone deeply enough into any path of life, or thought, or work; I had never had a cause to live for, and I might as well not have lived at all. If I have any faith left in me, it is that faith in a cause, as the soul, the grace, the beauty, the purpose of life.

I will seek then, I said to myself, a new activity. I will steep life in freshness, and re-colour it in the dyes of new sensations. *Ich will mein Glück probiren—marschiren!*

CHAPTER VIII.

YES; I began to think seriously of going to the United States, making my way out westward, buying land, and turning farmer. Vague and delightful visions of the forest scenery of the New World filled me; visions of woods where tints, which in our European region we know of only in manufactured colours, mingle and contrast in the living glory of the autumnal foliage. Dreams of the rolling prairie, and the deep wine-coloured brooklet, and the rushing river, were in my mind and before my senses. It seemed to me that nothing but the fresh bosom of the young mother-Nature of the West could revive my exhausted and flagging temperament. I was fast growing more and more weary of life as I found it and as I made it. Heat and crowd, and

midnight suppers, or lonely midnight grumblings
and reflections, perpetual excitement, fatigue,
overwork, too much wine, and the almost inces-
sant cigar,—these began to take effect just as I
might reasonably have expected. I found that
my voice already was beginning to show signs of
suffering. Nobody else noticed it yet; but I
could not be deceived. I consulted a medical
man, who recommended rest and country air;
and I thought of acting on his advice soon—some
time, perhaps, when the season was over, or next
year, or whenever convenient.

Meanwhile I went on as before; I mixed a
great deal with joyous company of all kinds. A
positive necessity for distraction of some sort
seemed to have seized hold of me, and it even
appeared as if distraction relieved my mind and
improved my physical condition. The resolve to
give up the stage and go to America, supplied a
delightful excuse and temptation. It would be
clearly a waste of power, an unnecessary vexation,
to put myself under heavy restraint just now,
when so short a time was to bring about a total

change of life and habits. The fresh manly life of the New World would soon restore me to that physical strength and brightness of temperament which I used to enjoy. No use, then, in beginning any reform before I undertake the enterprise which shall change scene and habits and life altogether.

I sometimes even thought of the expediency of marrying and ranging myself; taking a companion with me to America to be a backwoodsman's wife. But I always ended by dismissing the idea as one that brought up a sensation of repulsiveness with it. To begin with, I knew nobody whom I would or could marry. Most of the women I knew were singers or actresses; and I saw most of them too closely to be likely to fall in love with any, even if a deeper and earlier feeling did not absorb my heart. There was one to whom at times I did feel myself slightly attracted; she was the little Frenchwoman with whom I had had a sort of flirtation on the evening when I otherwise made a fool of myself at Christina's apartments. She did not discourage my attentions whenever they were offered, and I did sometimes pay court to her. She was young, and very pretty. She was not witty or intellectual, or gifted with any conversational power beyond what mere animal vivacity and flow of talk may give. I do not know why on earth I cared for her company, except that she was easy of access and full of life, and her society served to distract me, just as smoking or drinking might.

My new friend, who called herself Mdlle. Finola, and was the daughter, I came to know, of a fat couple who sold slippers in one of the passages of the Palais Royal, was a girl with a very agreeable light French sort of soprano voice, and pleasing vivacious ways, and an inordinate amount of self-conceit. She was not by any means a bad little person, and would rather, all things being equal, do a kindly thing than not. She was, I have no doubt, practically, or as Heine would say, anatomically, virtuous; but she had no particular prejudice in favour of virtue, and probably never troubled herself much by thinking on the subject.

Her ideas of life consisted of flattery, singing, lyrical successes, complimentary critiques in newspapers, jewels, crinoline (crinoline was rather a new fashion then), pleasant little dinners and suppers, carriages, and a fair prospect of a brilliant match. She had no more true lyrical genius than an Italian-boy's monkey; but she sometimes captivated audiences, and set them applauding with a genuine enthusiasm which Pasta might have failed to arouse. She had a quick arch way of glinting with her eyes, which conveyed to some people an idea of immense latent humour and *espièglerie*, that, I can answer for it, had no existence in my little friend's mental constitution. She turned her bright beaming orbs in flashing rapidity from stalls to boxes in a manner which irresistibly kept attention alive. Who could withdraw his interest for a moment from the stage when he could not tell but that the very next moment those glittering laughing brown eyes might roguishly seek out his own ? She had apparently the faculty of eye-flirting with every man in a whole theatre in turn. Then she shrugged her very full, white, and bare shoulders with such a piquancy, and had such quick graceful gestures, and so fluttered her pretty plumage, that it was quite a pleasant sight to see. Of course, all this told with much more decided effect in the Italiens, or some such house, than in one of our great temples of opera: but even in our vast house it had its effect upon the limited section from whom the rest of the audience, and the town generally, took their time.

Not, however, to be merely *piquante* and vivacious, Mdlle. Finola had a way of throwing a momentary gleam of tender softness into her eyes, and looking pensively before her, as if consciousness had withdrawn itself wholly from the audience, and buried itself in the depths of some sweet inner sadness; and she so trilled out a prolonged, plaintive, and dreamy note, that people sometimes declared her pathetic power quite equal to her humour and vivacity. When ordinary observers note any little effect produced with ease, they are apt to believe that the performer has a capacity for doing something infinitely greater, if he or she would only try, and did but care to succeed. A sad mistake generally; for on the stage and in real life we almost invariably do all we can and the best we can; and that which you see is the display of our whole stock of capability. But audiences could not readily believe that the one little bit of effective show had exhausted Mdlle. Finola's whole resources. The result was that in her own parts, Rosinas, Figlias del Reggimento, and so on, she was greatly admired, and her little tricks of instinctive coquetry and vivacity were accepted by many as the deliberate and triumphant efforts of graceful art, if not indeed the stray sparks which indicated the existence of a latent fire of true lyrical genius.

Now this little personage was beginning to be very popular about the time when Christina's husband came to London. She had not indeed come as yet into any sort of antagonism or rivalry with Madame Reichstein, and they never sang together; but Finola's nights were usually very successful, and she was even rallying a sort of party round her both in audiences and critics. Perhaps Christina's passionate enthusiastic style had begun to be too much for some of her hearers. True art is a sad strain upon the intellects of many of us ; and little Finola was a great relief. She was Offenbach after Meyerbeer; and a good many occupants of opera-stalls to-day know what that means, and can appreciate the charming relaxation to wearied inanity which it implies. And though not as yet anything of a rival to Christina, Finola was beginning to be talked about a good deal. I don't think Christina at this time cared in the least, or grudged the little thing any sprays of laurel that might fall to her. But she always affected to think me an admirer of Finola, one of Finola's party, and indeed, more than that, one of Finola's lovers; and at last, out of pure spleen at being so set down, I acted intentionally as if I were one of that silly throng; and as Mdlle. Finola liked flirting with anyone, she showed herself willing enough to flirt with me.

I have spoken of all this for the purpose of showing how matters stood as regarded Christina and myself just about the time when her husband made his appearance so unexpectedly in London. We—Christina and I—were on strange, cold, almost unfriendly terms, so far as all outer appearances went. My soul was still filled with love for her, wildly dashed sometimes with a bitterness not much unlike hate. She, on her side, seemed to me to be leading the life almost of a frivolous, careless, heartless coquette; I was drifting away from all my old moorings of steadfastness and perseverance and patience, and becoming an idler with the idle; I drank midnight, and thought midnight, as the phrase has it. With the sudden appearance of the Italian exile came a change in all our relationships; chance, utter chance, conspired with his own character and purpose, and the place he held in Christina's life, to make his presence the source of change and event to all of us.

In a very short time after his coming, Signor Salaris became the recognised lion of the London

season. He had, in the *impresario's* sense of
the word, quite a wonderful success. He delivered lectures on his imprisonment and his
escape, which crowded Willis's Rooms, and filled
King-street with coronetted carriages. He pleaded
the cause of his country; he called upon England to regard the independence of Italy as
Europe's most pressing and vital question; and
countesses clapped their kid-gloved hands and
waved their perfumed handkerchiefs. He dined
now with a Cabinet minister, and now with the
leader of the Opposition. He spent great part
of his time at Mr. Lyndon's. He was intrigued
for and battled for, as the attraction of evening-
parties. He bore it all patiently, as one who
does a work of drudgery with a good object; but
he smiled sadly and shook his head when one
congratulated him privately on his success. I
once told him he ought to be a proud man. He
said he felt profoundly discouraged. A great
illusion, he calmly said, was gone. England, he
now knew, would do nothing for his country.
He had come to plead for protection and help.

He found himself the hero of a carnival scene, pelted with flowers and sugar-plums.

I am not a politician, and this is not a political story. I introduce the subject of Salaris and his success, because at this time in one way, as later in another, it affected my own life.

I went one evening to hear my new friend tell his story and make his appeal in Willis's Rooms. I went alone; the room was crowded; Mr. Lyndon M.P. presided. There were present what Ned Lambert would have called "no end of swells." Salaris was speaking when I got in. He was really not, in the rhetorical sense, an eloquent man. He had nothing of Kossuth about him, nor had his style anything of the poetic grandiloquence of Mazzini. He talked in a simple, severe, unpretending sort of way, with hardly any gesticulation. The sincerity of his purpose, the clear straightforwardness of his language, the sweetness of his expression, made the great charm which, added of course to the romantic nature of his recent escape, delighted the West-end. He was a novelty in the way of exiles.

He positively seemed, I heard a lady near me remark, quite like an English gentleman. In fact, the Thaddeus of Warsaw personage was played out; and the West-end now thrilled with a new sensation, to see an escaped and exiled patriot who looked like an ordinary gentleman, and spoke as composedly as a financial member of Parliament.

I looked round the room, expecting to see Christina there. I was not disappointed. She was seated two or three rows of seats away from me, and she looked very handsome, but melancholy, and a little fatigued. She was apparently not listening much more attentively than I was. She saw me, and nodded a salutation, and whispered something to a lady at her side. The lady, who seemed to have been listening very closely to the speaker, looked up, and glanced towards me. She was very young—about nineteen, perhaps — with a delicate, clearly-shaped, youthful Madonna face, and eyes that had a tender violet light in them. They were eyes that did not flash or glitter or sparkle. They

rested on you with a quiet luminous depth, like
the light a planet seems to give. Her face had
a thoughtful, sweet, almost sad expression until
the violet light arising in the eyes suffused the
whole countenance with its genial radiancy. It
was a face not to be forgotten, once you had
seen it; and I had not forgotten it, for I had
seen it before, and had many a time wished to
see it again. It was the face of Mr. Lyndon's
youngest daughter; the girl to whom I had spoken
in Palace-yard when wild Stephen Lyndon made
his absurd mistake.

Did you ever, on an evening of reckless revelry,
amid an atmosphere steaming with heat and lights
and the fumes of wine, in a room ringing with
laughter and frivolity, suddenly open a window,
and looking out, catch a glimpse of the blue summer heaven and the pure light of the stars? If
so, you will understand how I felt when I looked
up from the increasing degeneracy of my life, with
its foolish excitements and its barren spasmodic
passion, and saw the face of Lilla Lyndon.

I glanced many times to where she sat, and I

forgot the cause of Italy's independence. Once, only once, she looked towards me.

There was a slight movement on the platform; a letter was handed to Mr. Lyndon. That gentleman said a word to the lecturer, who at once stopped, bowed, and drew back; and Mr. Lyndon, rising, came to the front and apologised for having to leave the chair. He was obliged to go down to the House immediately. His distinguished friend the Dean of some place or other, whose remarkable work recently published had proved how well he understood the Italian question and how thoroughly he sympathised with the cause of Italy, had kindly consented to take the chair. There was a murmur of genteel applause for Mr. Lyndon, another for the Dean, as the latter gracefully threw himself into the vacated chair; and then Mr. Lyndon disappeared from the platform, the lecture went on, and the audience settled itself to listen as before.

Once and only once did Salaris make any attempt at eloquence; and even that was but the eloquence of passionate conviction. It was at the close, where he proclaimed, rather than merely predicted, to his hearers that, let who would be friend or foe, the day of Italy's independence was sure and near. " Only yesterday," he said, " an English lady—I see her now in this room—gave me as an omen of good a translation of a noble poem by a great living poet, a German, which bids my country be of good cheer and expect her deliverance. Will you listen to a few lines? The German poet reminds my country of the story of Penelope: how she was fair, and persecuted for her beauty, and how the reckless strangers re-velled in her hall:

Twenty years the purple tissue span she weeping on her
    throne;
Twenty years in bitter sorrow nurtured her belovèd son;
Twenty years remained she faithful to her husband and her
    name—
Weeping, hoping, sending seekers—lo, and her Ulysses came!

Woe to the audacious wooers when they heard the avenger's
    tread,
And the bitter death-charged arrows from his clanging bow
    were sped;
With the red blood of the strangers hall and pavement drip
    ping lay,
And a fearful feast of vengeance then was held at Ithaca.

Knowest thou that song, Italia? Listen, and in patience wait,
Even although the swarm of strangers throng through thy
       ancestral gate;
Rear thy sons to fearless manhood, though with many a burn-
       ing tear;
Wait and hope; thy hour is coming; thy Ulysses too is near."

To the closing lines he gave all the dignity, the thrilling force, the strength of pathos and of hope, which the words deserved, and which his penetrating voice, his noble earnestness, his expression, now animated, could lend. "It is," he added slowly, " the poetry, the hope, the encouragement of a German ! *Quod minime reris !* The sympathy and the hope are the more welcome, the more delightful. I accept the omen for my country, and I say to her :

'Wait and hope; thy hour is coming; thy Ulysses too is near.'"

He remained for a moment motionless and silent, and the audience did not know whether he had finished or not; then his hand dropped upon the desk dear him, and he bowed to the as semblage, and drew back from the front of the platform. There was quite a cordial and enthusiastic demonstration of applause; and then began the rustling of silks, and calling of carriages, and the babble of talk with acquaintances, and the crowding on the stairs.

The moment the movement of departure began Madame Reichstein invited me by a look to come to her. She and Miss Lyndon had withdrawn into a corner a little out of the stream of the departing crowd. I made my way through groups of people and over trailing skirts to where they stood.

"How did you like it?" were Christina's first words; and then, without waiting for an answer, she said, "I wish to introduce you to Miss Lyndon—Miss Lilla Lyndon."

Before the ceremony of introduction was well through, two or three acquaintances closed round Madame Reichstein, and Miss Lyndon and I were left for the moment together.

"Am I wrong, Mr. Temple," she said, "in thinking that we have met and spoken together before?"

"No, Miss Lyndon, you are quite right."

"That day in Palace-yard, when that poor man

came up and stopped the carriage and called me by my name ?"

"That was the day. You have a good memory."

"It made a painful impression on me, that scene and that poor man. I thought I could not have been mistaken, Mr. Temple, in you, when I saw you a few nights ago for the first time since that day. May I congratulate you now on your success—on the name you have won since I first saw you? It always gave me pleasure to believe that it was you with whom I had spoken that day, for you were kind to that strange poor creature."

This was a subject that somewhat embarrassed me; I turned to something else.

"The lines that Signor Salaris recited were translated by you, Miss Lyndon, I venture to think ?"

"They were. Did you like them ?"

"I thought them noble in spirit, and I hope prophetic; and they sounded to me—I have not seen the original—like a pure and exquisite translation."

"I am very glad; they are Geibel's. They seemed to me prophetic, and so I showed them to Signor Salaris. He is a noble creature, and I hope whatever he engages in may succeed; but I don't understand much of Italian affairs."

"Nor I, indeed, Miss Lyndon."

"Not you? And yet you ought to be at least a sort of stepson of Italy."

"I only know my stepmother's voice. Her interests she keeps for her own children."

"We are going, Emanuel," said Christina, who was leaning on the arm of some gentleman.

I offered Miss Lyndon my arm, and she leaned on it: I felt the pressure of her light touch, and I was thrilled by it.

"Do you know, Mr. Temple," she said, as we descended the stairs, "I have never ceased to think that there was some mystery about that man in Palace-yard which I ought to know, and that *you* could explain it. How did he come to know my name, and why did his face seem so strange and yet so familiar to me? Will you tell me?"

"Pray, Miss Lyndon, don't ask me; I cannot tell you anything about him—at least not now; not without thinking over it. The secret, if it be one, may not be mine to tell."

"Then there is something?"

"There is."

"And he had some reason for knowing me and calling me by my name?"

"Pray don't ask any more. He had."

"I knew it," she said; and an unconscious vibration passed from her arm to mine.

"Some time, Miss Lyndon, you may know all; and it may be in your power to do good by the knowledge to people who are unhappy, and who don't deserve to be so."

She looked into my face, with surprise and deep interest in her clear pensive eyes.

Christina was already at the door of her little brougham waiting for us. I handed Miss Lyndon in. Christina gave me her hand without a word, and I saw a strange expression in her face, as if something had both perplexed and irritated her. I could not understand it.

Miss Lyndon held out her delicate little hand with a frank and friendly expression. I touched it, and the light pressure lingered long with me. As I left the place, I felt like one on whom the first breath of some purifying and sacred influence has fallen. The presence of this girl had strangely affected me when first I saw her, and I had never forgotten the sensation. Now it filled me almost wholly. It was indescribable; at least, I cannot describe it any better than by saying that while the presence of Christina seemed to allure me with the rich incense of flowers, that of Lilla Lyndon made me thoughtful and full of pure regret and humility, like the light of the stars.

In most stories of ghosts and demons and warlocks, is it not sufficient to speak of the odious and supernatural creature in order to evoke his presence? Apparently some spell of the same kind haunted me this night. Miss Lyndon and I had spoken of the man who accosted her in Palace-yard; I had never seen him since my return from Italy. I had hardly got a dozen paces

from the door of Willis's Rooms when I came
straight on him.

Keeping the same side as you walk from
Willis's Rooms towards St. James's-square, you
may see as you look across the street a row of
white and stuccoed houses on the other side, one
of which has a fame attached to it. When I
nearly fell over Stephen Lyndon, he was standing on the edge of the footpath, looking up at
that particular house. He did not seem a day
older than when I saw him last. He wore the
black wig as before, and was rather better dressed
than I had seen him on some former occasions,
though not up to the mark of one memorable
occasion when he came out resplendent. It
seemed to me, too, that there was a little more
of quietness and caution about him than was his
wont in earlier times.

I did not know then that he was there waiting
for me. So I felt vexed when I nearly ran up
against him, and recognised him in the clear
moonlight of a beautiful night, and saw that he

had recognised me, and there was no escape
without at least a parley.

"Good - evening, Temple," he said in the
coolest and easiest kind of way, as if we had
met only the night before last; and he quietly
laid his hand on my arm and stayed my going
farther. "I have been contemplating that house
over there; the first of the row. I have been
meditating, Temple. An exile lived there once,
my child of song—an illustrious exile. Where is
he now, Temple? Only on a throne, my swan.
There are exiles and exiles, Temple. Our patrio-
tic and banished friend Salaris will hardly, I
think, come to so brilliant a place. The throne
for one conspirator, and the prison or very likely
the block for another. Crowns for the crowns
that have brains under them; blocks for the
blockheads. He is a gifted and touching block-
head, that friend of ours, Mr. Temple. I like
him; but I was always a child of sentiment. I
saw *you* in Willis's Rooms."

"Were you there?"

"I was there; O yes. He and I, you know,

are old friends. I saw Goodboy on the platform, and he saw me. I think he winced a little, but it was a lost fear. I have given up my notion of doing anything with him in the way of street-scenes."

"I am very glad to hear it. I do hope you have turned decent and honourable and manly. Mr. Lyndon, there are many reasons why I wish you well."

"Thanks; I daresay. I really believe you, Temple; and I think you are a good sort of fellow in your way. Yes, I am quite a reformed man. In fact, Temple, he was too much for me that way."

"What way?"

"You never heard, then?"

"I have not heard anything about you for a long time."

"True; you were away in Italian myrtle-bowers, and that sort of delightful thing. Well, I opened fire regularly on Goodboy; waylaid him at his door; pursued him to the House, to the Club, to the Opera. What do you think he did?

He coolly took the bull by the horns. He gave me in charge to a policeman; he followed up the charge at the police-court; he delivered his version of the business with a dignified mock humility which quite touched and charmed 'the worthy magistrate.' He recounted all the things he had done for me, and all our venerable father had done; and it was a magnificent scene, quite. And do you know, Temple, while the whole thing was a hideous lie from beginning to end, there was not a word in it which was not literally true? It put me in an unpleasant light; that I must frankly confess. Well, there was nothing for me but to find bail—which of course I couldn't do—or be sent to prison, or pledge my honour to molest him no more—in that way. Temple, I was defeated. I had fought Respectability, and was overthrown! At least, I had the sense to know that I was beaten, and I surrendered and promised."

"I am very glad to hear it."

"Are you? So, I daresay, is Goodboy. But wait for the end. Do you ever read the Greek

dramatists, Temple? I suppose not. Well, there
is some good advice given by one of them about
counting no man successful until you have seen
the game all out. You just wait. If I detested
Goodboy before, do you think I like him any
better now? Do you know, the cunning old boy
managed so well, that not a line of the business
got into the papers; so that I had not even the
satisfaction of bringing open scandal on him. I
wrote letter after letter to the papers; need I say
that no editor did me the favour of putting the
tale of the wrongs I had suffered into print? Well,
there's enough of that. I have had rather a hard
life of it since. Give you my word, I don't think
anything could have kept me up but my deep religious feeling and my determination to be revenged
upon my enemies. I thought it well to retire
from the metropolis for a little. I broke loose
from my base, and marched right into the heart
of the country—Liverpool, Manchester, and that
sort of place. Coarse, cloddish, without soul,
without humour, and, let me tell you, by no
means green or awkward with the cards and the

billiards. Ah, *mon Dieu!* it was hard and dull.
No matter, I live! Providentially preserved, I
still live! I return to town at last, led doubtless
by my star. I find two of my old acquaintances
established as lions of the season. You are one;
my Carbonaro of Willis's Rooms is the other.
Good Heaven, it ought to teach the vainest of us
a lesson in modesty, when such people can be
successful."

We were now walking round St. James's-
square. We might have been mistaken for two
dear and intimate friends. Lyndon was leaning
affectionately on my arm, even when he was
propounding lessons of humility drawn from the
incomprehensible fact that such a personage as I
had succeeded.

I thought of him then as I had thought of
him always since our first meeting—as a hopeless
old reprobate, whose inner nature no power on
earth could touch, and whose utterly selfish and
heartless levity could only be explained or excused
by the theory that something not unlike insanity
was mingled with his blood. Yet I now walked

with him, listened to him, allowed him to lean on me, felt even a positive interest in his welfare.

Why? Was it for the sake of Ned Lambert and his love, and my sincere friendship for them both?

In sad sober truth, it was not.

It was because the thoughtful violet eyes of Lilla Lyndon the younger had looked into mine with kindly interest while she spoke of this man. The thought of her transfigured him in my mind. Nay, this miserable wretch was a sort of link between us. His very misery might be the cause of our meeting again.

And at this time I had no more thought of loving Lilla Lyndon than I had of falling in love with a saint or a star. I still believed that my life was to be for ever shadowed and frustrated by hopeless unfading passion for Christina Reichstein.

I listened, then, to Lyndon's talk, and even encouraged him, and assured him I would save him if I could.

"Now that," he said, "is the very thing I am coming at. I really do think, Temple, that you are a sincere sort of person; and that you mean what you say. My daughter has disappeared somewhere; I cannot find out where: and I don't suppose, you know, that it much matters, because I daresay the girl is hard up, and drudging and toiling, and that sort of thing, and of course she couldn't do anything for me. I should think Goodboy turned her adrift; he's quite mean enough for it. Well, you see, it's no use my looking her up. Do you know, I am so sensitive, and epicurean, and chivalrous in all my ways, that I can't bear to see women who are drudging and poor and overworked. It isn't the poetic idea of womanhood, is it? Women don't look as if they ought to be seen then. They get pale and washed-out-looking, and the plump outlines go, and their hands look dirty and needle-marked, and all the rest of it. No; I really prefer, as a father, not to see my daughter just now. You follow me, Temple?"

"I do," was my grim reply. Even the colour of those violet eyes was fading from my mind as he talked in this way.

" You appreciate what I mean ?"

" Quite," I replied more grimly.

" Now, on the other hand, look at my niece.
Aha, have I touched you?" I suppose I started.
" There is a lovely girl, charming to look at; a
little pale, you will say; but so very interesting,
and with such an expression of goodness. Now,
Temple, don't you think *she* could be brought to
do something for me? Don't you think, at least,
she ought to be allowed to know of my existence?
I know it's kept a secret from her. I know she is
ignorant of the tender tie that binds her to me.
Now, Temple, my boy, here is your opportunity!
You know her; you are in your own way a kind
of success, and I daresay would pass off easily
upon her—she's evidently very green and innocent
—as quite a distinguished and delightful sort of
person. I saw you handing her to the carriage
to-day; you did the thing quite in good style; I
daresay she wouldn't notice any difference. Now,
your motive cannot be suspected. Mine, I confess, is open to misinterpretation! Temple, do a
benevolent deed. Here is an outcast uncle pant-

ing for love and redemption, and very, very hard up. There is a lovely niece, with her little bosom overflowing with family affection and benevolence and romantic nonsense of all kinds, and with unlimited influence over papa's purse, Temple, need I say more? You have a heart, and quite a presentable appearance. Bring us together, and look for your reward Above."

I managed to escape at last, without making a promise of any kind; but he squeezed my hand warmly, accepted a trifling loan, and went away humming a hopeful tune.

CHAPTER IX.

RIVALRY.

Our season was drawing fast to a close—the first season during which Christina and I had sung together—the season of fruition! I had some continental engagements during the winter; she intended to take absolute rest, for she had been apparently in uncertain and even delicate health for some time back, and her voice had occasionally failed her. Just at the close of the season, she brought on herself, by want of caution, rather a severe attack of chest or throat complaint, as shall be presently told.

Her husband had left London, disappointed but not dispirited. He was in Paris, striving to teach diplomatists and statesmen there the necessity of doing just what was afterwards done; that

is to say, boldly and in the field taking up the
cause of Italy against Austria. As yet his efforts
did not promise much success, and of England
he had no longer any hope.

On the very day after the Willis's-Rooms lecture at which I was present, Christina was at-
tacked by a sort of nervous weakness and cold,
and her place was vacant for a week. Mdlle.
Finola made her hay while the sun shone, and
came out prominently. Crowded houses and animated audiences greeted her, and she began to
walk the stage with an air of conquering rivalry
in the very rustle of her petticoats. Critiques
were written, proclaiming her the mistress of a
new style, the leader of a new lyrical school.
She took all the praises with a quiet *nonchalance*,
as if they were nothing but the homage properly
due to genius. To crown the whole, she under-
took some of Christina's own favourite parts, and
produced a curious half-pathetic half-comic *mé-
lange*, which it was not possible to think uninter-
esting, kept people's eyes and ears quite open,
puzzled many intelligent and appreciative lis-

teners, and was hailed with positive enthusiasm by the general public.

I had to sing with Mdlle. Finola in most of her parts; and at first I put on a kind of high-art indifference towards the whole affair. Indeed, I did not care to sing with any woman but Christina, and I looked upon little Finola as a mere musical stop-gap. But her triumph fairly startled me; and the evident dissatisfaction of some of the audience at my own careless performance, together with some sharp reprimands from the fair singer herself, piqued and roused me at last into animation. I determined to enter into the spirit of the thing, and play my part in the admirable fooling. I sang and acted my very best, reproached my white-robed Amina (whose stage night-dress was a masterpiece of elaborate millinery such as no princess ever went to bed in) with all the tones of despair and jealous madness; clasped my plump and tightly-laced Leonora, and sighed out to the uttermost my passionate farewell. I was graciously permitted by my conquering heroine to share the honours of her triumph;

I led her forth; I seized as many of her bouquets as two hands could grasp; I held back the curtain that she might squeeze her ample skirts through—she wore crinoline even when Amina in the bedroom—I attended her to her brougham, and was admitted to a gracious degree of her patronage and favour.

"I don't think the world misses Madame Reichstein so much," she remarked to me one evening.

"I don't think it does," I added, with a bitter conviction that it was only too true.

"You see," she went on complacently, and with a quite judicial calmness and self-satisfaction; "it wearies soon, that grand lyricism of the old school. The world will have vivacity and *esprit*. One must suit the public; but one must have tact to do it. For me, I never admired Madame Reichstein; and I know she always detested me."

"Indeed you do her wrong; I have always heard her speak very well of you."

"Possible; but that was before she thought I

could be a rival. One does not like a rival, especially when one is not very young. She will soon be quite *passée*, I think. How old is she?"

"I really don't know," I replied rather coldly.

"Truly? I thought you knew her whole history. She cannot be much less than forty."

"O yes, certainly, very much less than forty; not more than thirty, perhaps."

"Then you do know something of her? I always heard that you did. Yes, I heard that you were in love with her ever so long ago—before I was born, perhaps—and that she married somebody else, who was killed, or died, or ran away; and lately I heard that you had arranged your old quarrel, and were going to marry her; but I did not believe that."

This was all hideously annoying; and nothing but the sense I had of the absurdity which would attach to a dispute with such a girl, who, after all, talked no worse than most women will do of rivals, prevented me from giving some sort of distinct expression to my feelings.

Mdlle. Finola read my face and laughed.

"*Allons!*" she said, "you are angry with me because I mock myself of your old love. I believe she is more jealous of me now than ever."

"Come, now, mademoiselle, don't be foolish. You are not ill-natured, I know, and you ought not to talk spiteful nonsense of that sort."

"Perhaps. But when a woman has carried a high head over one for a long time, it is a grand provocation to be spiteful. Without doubt, she has said as much or more of me since these last few days : but I will say not one word more if you are hurt; and don't quarrel with me, for I meant no harm ; and if I had known it would touch you, I never would have said a word against her—*du moins* in your presence."

That night we were singing together in the *Trovatore*, which used to be such a favourite then; and the audience were even more than usually delighted with the astonishing little Leonora. After one of her thrilling passages (which reminded me of a canary-bird in love), the beautiful Leonora passing me quickly said, with a beam of self-satisfaction twinkling in her bright eyes, "*She* is in the house."

I had no need to ask whom she meant. I saw Christina in a box. She was very pale, and looked worse than I should have expected.

I called to see her next day, and ventured to reproach her for coming out at night so soon; but she made no answer on that subject.

"You sang very well last night," she said; "with more soul than you generally throw into your parts."

"Did I really? I was afraid I was getting through in a blank and careless kind of way. What did you think of Leonora?"

I asked the question with some doubt, unwilling to ask it, but not seeing how to avoid it. I expected some sarcastic or contemptuous answer, or some transparent affectation of admiration.

"I was both surprised and pleased with her," Christina answered with perfect composure and apparent earnestness. "There is something quite new and fresh about her style, which makes her very interesting. I never thought she had so much originality. She quite inspired *you*."

"Did she? I am glad to be inspired by anybody, or in any way."

"You don't sing so well with me. Why?"

"Perhaps because I strive to do my best too anxiously. Besides, your genius rebukes me, Christina; that is the truth. You are too true an artist for me; I don't care about little Finola."

"People say you do, in another sense."

"Do you believe them?"

"No, Emanuel, not I.—What do you think of Mr. Lyndon's daughter?"

She looked at me fixedly while she put this utterly inappropriate question.

"She is a beautiful girl, and I should think she must have a beautiful nature. How came such a father to have such a daughter?"

"You dislike Mr. Lyndon, and cannot judge of him. Now *I* don't dislike Lilla."

"No; why should you?"

"Some women one could dislike, others one could not. I could not dislike your little friend

Finola; I should as soon think of disliking a clever linnet. No matter; let us pass all that. You must sing your very best with me on Monday."

"Next Monday? You surely don't mean to sing next Monday?"

"Indeed I do."

"Is that not rashness?"

"Very likely. I mean to do it, though."

"Pray, Christina, don't attempt it. Do let me advise you—"

"My dear friend, I never take advice. My voice is quite restored, and I mean to sing on Monday. Do you think I am going to allow the season to close with your little friend in full possession?"

"You don't fear rivalry. Your place is always yours to resume when you will."

"Still, you don't know what woman's vanity is, if you think I could be content to endure a six months' exile from London with the knowledge that I had left your fascinating friend in possession of the field. No; I must win a battle before I

go. Besides, I want to sing with you again; I
want to be certain whether you cannot sing as
well with me as with her."

While we were speaking, there was heard a
trampling of horses in the street below; and in a
moment a card was brought to Christina. When
she looked at it, she glanced at me suddenly, and
with a sort of flush in her face, as if I were somehow concerned in the matter.

"No, I can't see her," she said to her German
companion. "Yet, stay; it's very kind of her.
Yes; show her into the other room, Meta."

I rose to go.

"One moment, Emanuel; oblige me by re-
maining one moment. I wish it particularly."

I remained; standing up, however.

Presently I heard the rustle of skirts up the
stairs and in the next room.

"Now, Emanuel," said Christina with an odd
and embarrassed kind of half-smile, "you are free
to go. No; you need not advise or remonstrate;
it would be useless. I mean to resume my place

on Monday, and dethrone your little friend, or perish in the attempt."

She laughed a somewhat forced and flickering laugh, and I left.

Who was her mysterious visitor, whom I was not to pass on the stairs even; for that was clearly the reason why Christina had detained me? Well, there could not be much mystery on the part of the visitor. As I came into Jermyn-street I saw a mounted groom leading a lady's horse up and down before the door. I knew the man's face perfectly well; he was one of Mr. Lyndon's servants. The visitor was evidently Lilla Lyndon.

CHAPTER X.

A DEFEAT.

CHRISTINA carried out her resolve, and sang the following Monday night in one of the parts to which Mademoiselle Finola had given a new reading. When she came on the stage she looked weak, I thought, and nervous. I could not see her without deep and genuine emotion. I could not but think of our early acquaintance and our early love; of the promises we had made to each other of a happiness never given us to enjoy; of the bright assurance of success which always sustained her, and of the success she had won, and the slender joy it seemed to have brought her. I felt the keenest sense of delight when I heard the enthusiastic welcome she received from the house, and saw her eyes sparkle with triumph; and yet

I could not help pitying her, because she loved so
much a triumph like that.

She sang exquisitely in the first act,—not,
indeed, with all her wonted strength, as my quick
and watchful ear soon discovered, but with all the
soul of feeling and the perfection of articulation
which belonged specially to her.   Her rival's performance must have seemed, in the mind of any
cultivated listener, a poor and tricky piece of arti-
ficiality when compared with her pure, noble,
lyrical style.   I saw her in the interval after the
first act, and she was full of triumph.

"Come," she said, "I have not been so rash,
after all; I have not failed, you see.   I know you
are glad of it, even though people do rank you on
the side of your pretty Mademoiselle Finola."

"Nobody can sing as you can; and for the
rest, you are only laughing at me."

"Perhaps so.   Indeed, I feel in exuberant
spirits to-night; partly, of course, because I have
got back my voice, and am about to recover my
place, but still more because I have had good
news."

"Indeed! when?" I knew by her expression that she was alluding to her husband.

"To-day. Everything is going well. He hopes to be able presently to take a little rest at Vichy; and I am going there."

"But what is going well? for I know nothing."

"*Ach!* nor I much more. But he has some enterprise in preparation, and it is going well, and he is hopeful. One may rely upon him, for he is not sanguine or extravagant; he is not a dreamer, though many people think him so. It was quite miserable to me to have to lie on a sofa all day long up there in Jermyn-street, with nothing to do but torture my brains and my heart thinking something had befallen him. But things look brighter now. I am very well now—don't you think so?"

"I would rather not see you here to-night. I doubt whether you are strong enough even yet."

"Strong enough! Quite. I could not be better. You don't think my voice was weak?"

"No; but even now you seem nervous, and look pale."

"Only because I am full of hope and triumph."

Our conversation was cut short just then, and I was a *primo uomo* once more.

I was glad when the opera was finished. It was a weary and a painful business to me, and to more than me. Christina's triumph was not long-lived. A vague sense of languor and of weakness began to diffuse itself through the house during the second act. It became very plain that Christina had tried her strength too soon, and was not equal to the task she had so rashly set herself. It was not that she decidedly failed, but that she did not keep up her success. The music of the part became an effort to her. She grew more and more dispirited. In my anxiety that her wish for a triumph should be gratified, I would have welcomed even some sudden expression of dissatisfaction from the house, because that would probably have fired her into energy. Of course nothing of the kind was heard. The house was thoroughly sympathetic and respectful. I knew how bitter to her would be even that sympathetic respectfulness; for it was the softened shadow of failure where she had expected to be illumined by the full blaze of success.

"She's not herself at all to-night," said somebody to me during a momentary meeting. "She ought not to have sung."

"She ought not indeed," I said very blankly.

"I thought she was going to make a splendid thing of it at first; but it is quite plain that she is not equal to it. I am very sorry she made the attempt, for it will be a sort of triumph to little Finola and her clique. Have you seen her to-night? There she is, yonder in that box, seemingly enjoying the whole affair—the little musical humbug."

I could not help smiling at the vigorous truthfulness with which he analysed the character of Mademoiselle.

"People have been telling me," he went on, "that you were going over to her party. No truth in that, I should think?"

"Not one solitary word of truth in it."

"No; I hardly thought you could mistake that musical-snuff-box sort of thing for singing, and those winks and shrugs for acting. I am very sorry for Reichstein, but it's only just a moment's disappointment. Let her keep quiet and recover her strength, and she'll extinguish little robin redbreast yonder."

The extinguishing, however, was not destined to take place that night. Christina's voice failed her more and more. The performance dragged through lifelessly and sadly. She could not sing.

When all was over, I found her far more calm and self-controlled than I had expected.

"I have made a complete failure of it," she said.

"It was too soon for you to attempt singing; that was all. There was no question of failure."

"I ought to have taken your advice from the first; but I was so confident of success. I suppose everyone perceived that I was not able to get through with it?"

"Everyone knew of course that you had not

been well, and no one expected to find that you had fully recovered your voice so soon."

" I saw your friend, Mademoiselle Finola. No doubt she thinks the victory is hers now—and indeed it is. Is it not, Emanuel?"

" You have only been defeated by yourself, because you would not do yourself justice."

" I ought to have taken your advice in the matter, for it must have been disinterested. If what people say be true, you ought to be glad that I persisted in singing, and failed accordingly."

I bit my lips, and felt hurt and vexed by allusions, of which I could not affect to misunderstand the meaning. This was no time, however, to take offence at any word of Christina's.

" You have not seen her since?" she proceeded, with a determined and vexing purpose. " Why don't you go to her and congratulate her on her triumph?"

" I had better," I could not help answering, "go to her or to anyone who will be less ungenerous and will understand me better than you do, Christina."

"But don't go, please, just yet. I do wrong to speak in that way, Emanuel, for I don't believe one word they say about your being leagued against me with her—I could not believe it. But I cannot help being vexed and spiteful after such a failure, and under her very eyes. Are you not sorry to see me so weak and vain?"

"I am, Christina; I do think such ways unworthy of you. What rivalry can there be between you and that little creature? Let her enjoy her triumph, if she thinks it one. You know what it means, and what it is worth, and how long it is likely to last. It's a shame, Christina; you have other things to think of besides her and her clique and their trumpery gossip."

"I have indeed; and I deserve to be reminded of it. You were always like an honest doctor, Emanuel—a doctor who does not mind giving his patient a little extra pain, if he can do any good by it. But you must forgive a little vexation to one who comes out for a great victory, and goes home defeated. You will come and sup with us? We were to have had a celebration of my triumph; now it shall be a feast of condolence. Come; and I promise not to say another word about Finola."

" Say anything you like about her, *meinet-wegen;* but don't sink yourself even for a moment to her level."

" Well, will you come ? I thought of dismissing my guests; but I will not do so if you will come."

" Let me refuse. Do not have guests. You are not fit for midnight, and talk, and excitement. Send them away."

" Ah, but I am sadly in want of a flash of excitement now. Do come, Emanuel; there are only to be a few. Mr. Lyndon—"

" No, Christina; forgive me, if I say point-blank, I don't want to meet that man, and least of all in your company. I dislike him, and I wish I could get you to do the same."

" Thanks. Our feelings are not likely to run quite in the same channel as regards the Lyndon family, I fancy. Meanwhile Mr. Lyndon is my friend and my husband's. Then you will not come? Good-night."

" You are offended with me ?"

" A little, and justly; but I quite forgive you; only let us say no more about it. And so good-night."

This conversation took place before we were out of the opera-house. I left her, and went my way alone.

Walking homewards an hour after, I passed through Jermyn-street. Coming near Christina's lodgings, I could not help thinking over the strange mixture of levity and feeling, of egotism and generosity, of ambition and frivolity, which was in that singular nature; ambition so great and jealousies so small; success discoloured by such petty bitternesses; great hopes made mean by such little pleasures and excitements. I wished she had sought solitude, not society, that night. I could not bear to think of her making one at a small revelry, and accepting, and perhaps enjoying, the attentions of Mr. Lyndon. Not my Lisette !

I might have spared myself some of these reflections. When I came in sight of her windows, there were no signs of revelry of any sort; all was quiet and dark. She had evidently got rid of her guests, and gone home to solitude.

"I don't understand this woman yet," I thought. "For good or ill, I don't understand her. I wonder if I ever shall. Are any women ever to be understood at all?"

Christina sang no more that season, of which indeed but few nights remained. She had attempted too much and too soon, and had to bear the penalty—bitter to her—of enforced rest.

I did not see her any more that year. I called many times, but she could not or would not see me. After a few weeks she went to Vichy, and thence to Nice. I had several provincial and some German engagements, and our paths divided altogether for many months.

So closed our first season—for her in disappointment; for me in disappointment of more than one kind. One thing was clear; Christina and I were far more widely separated now than when she was struggling in Italy, and I struggling in London, and neither knew of the other's whereabouts.

Let me dispose, once for all, of Mademoiselle Finola, who is of no further importance in this story, and need not appear in it any more. She had troops of admirers and many adorers; and among the latter she soon found an eligible husband. He was a man of large property and with a foreign title. She renounced the stage right joyously, and betook herself to an existence of balls and receptions, in which her soul found higher delight and more fitting sphere than it could have discovered in any triumph of musical art. Her name has been forgotten among singers long ago; and she is not sorry. She carried off at the very outset the only prize she cared about; and she looked back ever after on her artistic career as one remembers the weary progress of a journey which has led him to the warmth and light of a happy home. She lived principally

in London, not much caring to go back to Paris
while the shoe-shop still stood in the Palais-
Royal arcade. I met her several times after her
marriage, and she was very friendly and gracious
for awhile, until chance and change gradually
brought us less and less within each other's
sight, and at last extinguished even recognition.

The first season, then, in which Christina and
I sang together had come and gone; and this was
what it brought. I knew no end of people now,
and I doubt if London held a lonelier man. I
felt as if I were running to seed; and I longed
for a new life—a new start in life. It came;
but not in the way I had planned or expected.
The unforeseen, as usual, came to pass.

CHAPTER XI.

ANOTHER season opens, finding everything with me much the same, to all outward appearance, as the season before. I have not yet carried out my idea of going to America; and just at the present moment the idea is rather in the background. I have been in London since before Christmas, and the spring is now well advanced. I am still lodging under the same roof with Ned Lambert, though we sometimes don't meet for weeks together. I hear rather promising accounts of the poor Lyndons in Paris. I have not seen Christina, or heard from her all the winter; but I know that she has been to Nice, and that Mr. Lyndon, M.P., has been there, without his daughters; and I know what the English colony there said and thought, and, while I believe it to be false as hell, I am maddened by such whispers. I know the common talk here is that Christina is to marry Lyndon; and I wish her husband would abandon his conspiracies, and own his wife, and live with her in the face of day. I have heard something from him too; and news of him. There has been an abortive insurrection in Lombardy, and a few poor fellows have been bayoneted and shot, and some people blame Salaris for it, and say that he was there; and others condemn Mazzini, and say that *he* was not there.

Christina's engagement here, beginning rather late this year, is near at hand, and she must soon be in town. I have heard that her voice is quite restored, but that her general health is still weak.

One morning I receive a letter addressed to me in her handwriting. I see it with something like a start. The time has been my whole senses would have stirred at the sight of that writing; and even still I cannot look at it unmoved. I believe there are some early feelings one never gets over—never. I shall never conquer my detestation of the smell of certain medicines. The faintest breath of them horrifies me, as if I were again a child about to have a dose forced down my throat. I shall never lose a sense of delight called up by the smell of tar; because it brings back all the old memories of the sea and the strand and the boats. I shall never see a scrap of Christina Braun's handwriting without emotion. There are no particular mysteries to be treasured up to the end of this story, and I may say at once that I love another woman now better than I ever loved the idol of my boyhood. But I can look at her writing in a letter without anything of a thrill, while a line of Christina Braun's hand would even still produce at the first glance a sort of electric shock.

Christina's letter was short.

"Jermyn-street.

"MY DEAR EMANUEL,—Greeting! I have returned to town, as you will see, and I want to speak to you frankly, earnestly, as a friend. Do you believe me a true friend, above meanness, and wishing you well? If so, forget any little coldness or ill-humour I may have shown last year, when I was troubled so much mentally and physically, and come to me at once. If you do not thus believe in me, then tear up this letter, and don't come.

"CHRISTINA."

I went to Jermyn-street immediately. Christina's German companion received me at first; and in a few minutes Christina herself entered. She was looking rather pale, but very handsome, and bright-eyed, and splendid.

"I am glad you have come," she said; "it is friendly of you. I wished to speak to you a little." And she glanced at the other woman, who was still in the room.

"First of yourself, Madame Reichstein. You are recovered — really recovered and strong, I hope."

"O yes, I think so. I was not very well all the winter; and many things made me uneasy and distressed."

She looked at me with such an expression

that I knew she referred to her husband. Indeed, I believe her German companion was quite in her confidence on this point.

"But I am better now—much better; quite restored, I think. And Finola is married, and has a title, and is happy! And Ned Lambert is not married, and is not happy! I saw poor Ned the other day in Paris; dear good Ned! He is not happy—and he is uneasy about some of his friends."

Here Christina lifted her eyes and let them rest full on me, as if she would read my very heart. I don't think I met the gaze quite boldly.

"Did you meet many friends in Nice?" I asked, not knowing anything else to say.

"Some; not many. Mr. Lyndon was there part of the time."

"So I heard."

I now looked fixedly at Christina in my turn. She did not wince.

"I believe," she said quite carelessly, "some people say Mr. Lyndon and I are to be married. —What do you think of that story, Meta?"

Meta smiled a dry smile.

"Herr Lyndon is *ein bischen alt*—a little old," was her only remark; and in a moment or two, to my great relief, she left the room, and I prepared to hear what Christina had to say.

When Meta was present, Christina had been sitting on a music-stool, while I sat quite away on a chair near the window. When we were left alone, she rose and stood near the fireplace, where, bright spring day though it was, there were blazing embers, and she motioned to me to come near.

I came and stood close beside her.

"I have asked you to come," she said, "to speak of you, not of me."

I suppose that was a note of defiance in reply to my look when we spoke of Mr. Lyndon.

There was nothing indeed I wished to say or to hear said on the subject of Mr. Lyndon and his attentions, or the talk they created. I merely bowed my head in token of assent.

Then Christina, throwing back her hair with one hand, and looking fixedly at me for an instant or two, said:

"Now, Emanuel, I have something earnest to say to you. Just a word or two of question and of warning. You will take both question and warning in a friendly spirit, will you not?"

I think I now knew what was coming, although the reader does not. 1 fear I flushed a little; but I answered calmly,

"Surely, Christina, I could not receive any word from you but as a friend."

"I thank you for the confidence. Now for the word, Emanuel. What about Lilla Lyndon?"

"About Lilla Lyndon! Which Lilla Lyndon? There are two."

Christina shook her head.

"Not worthy of you, Emanuel. Evasion to no purpose. Tell me to mind my own affairs, and leave you to yours, and I will do so. But if you allow me to be your friend, and admit confidence, don't evade. I have always confided in you."

"I don't think you have."

"So far as I could just now. I have told you there are certain things I cannot quite explain even yet, but that they shall be explained. I have never evaded your questions. I once rather anticipated them—put them for you and gave the answers, so far as any question might be given. Now, have you not been evading my question? Did you not understand it? Did I not see in your face that you understood it?"

"Well, Christina, I suppose I did. It is no use trying to evade so keen a questioner; and I wish I had answered you directly at once, and not given an appearance of mystery where there is none, and no need of any. Come, put any question you will—only don't expect that anything mysterious or romantic or interesting is likely to come in the way of answer."

"Well, then, again: what about Lilla Lyndon?"

"I can only say, so far as I know, nothing. To Lilla Lyndon I am nothing. To me she is a sweet, calm, pure-hearted creature, who seems to come out of dreamland, or poetry, or some old chronicle of saints—and that is all."

"How long have you known her?"

"Comparatively speaking, a short time. The

first time I ever saw her, and spoke to her, was before I went to Italy, and I then saw her hardly five minutes. Last season I saw her with you, as you will remember. Since I came back, I—I did meet her again."

" That is, you threw yourself in her way ?"

"I did ; but not for any purpose of my own. I threw myself in her way because I thought I saw through her a means of helping and serving two dear friends—you know them both—Ned Lambert and Lilla, the other Lilla, Lyndon. Most truly can I say I did not selfishly do this ; but I did it, and this was how our acquaintance began."

" All that I knew."

" Then that is all."

" No, not nearly all. You have met her lately ?"

" I have."

" And often ?"

" Yes, often."

" In plain words, you have met this girl regularly, by appointment with her, in Kensington-gardens ?"

" No, Christina, that is not so. Whoever told you that part of the story, told you what was not true, what was flatly false ; and if it were a man, I should like to have a chance of saying as much to him. One word of this kind never passed between us. We never met by appointment. I am not so mean as to think of such a thing ; and if I had suggested it, I must have been answered just as I deserved."

" Well, I hear all this with pleasure—with some pleasure, at least. But you have met several times, quite by accident, as she walked in Kensington-gardens. She has stopped and spoken to you at the railings as she rode in the Row."

" She has : and to many others too."

" Yes; the recognised friends of her family; her father's friends."

I felt myself flushing with anger. I wish I could have felt myself clear enough of conscience to reply.

" Come, Emanuel, again let me quote *Zwischen uns sei Wahrheit*. You have deliberately put yourself in the way of meeting Miss Lyndon?"

"I have."

"And you have met her so often and so regularly, that you can nearly always count upon meeting her on certain days in the same place. This is true?"

"It is true."

"And she is—well, not to be hard upon your years, which would seem painfully like being hard on my own—she is at least fourteen or fifteen years younger than you—is, in fact, considerably under age?"

"She is."

"And you think you are acting honourably in this?"

"I do not!" I exclaimed, so suddenly and sharply that Christina drew back a little, and glanced uneasily at the door, as if fearful lest we should have been overheard. "I do not, Christina! I count it dishonourable—frankly dishonourable. I have been ashamed of myself long enough for doing it. When a poor boy in a small seaport, I would not have done so. But I have changed, and life has been dull and lonely to me, and I did like to meet that sweet pure girl, who seemed to me something so unlike the common world, that her very presence brightened life to me. And I am afraid I liked it none the less because I detested that cold-blooded, sensuous, selfish old hypocrite, her father."

"Hush, hush, Emanuel, you don't know Mr. Lyndon—you and he seem, I can't tell how, to have a sort of instinctive aversion to each other."

"No; I don't suppose he even honours me with his aversion—and I don't care."

"Then let him pass; come to his daughter. I think I am satisfied, Emanuel. I think, as you look this thing so fearlessly in the face and don't spare yourself, you need no farther appeal—no appeal from me; still, I meant to give you a warning. Let me give it before you leave; we shall not often have such confidential conversations. Emanuel, do you love this girl?"

I turned away, and walked to the window. Christina came to me, and laid her hand upon my shoulder.

"Speak frankly to me—as to your friend or your sister. Do you love her?"

"Can *you* ask such a question?"

"O yes. Gone is gone, my friend, and dead is dead. I don't expect that the past could live for ever in your heart, and I should be sorry if it did. Let us remember nothing but so much as may give us a right to trust in each other. You do, then, love her?"

Christina's voice trembled a little as she spoke.

"Christina, I have not thought of loving her; not in that sense. Not as I loved you—not as I—"

"Then why do you meet her?"

"Because I was lonely, and at odds with everything, and her voice sounded sweetly in my ears, and her eyes looked kindly on me; and she was a mild delightful influence, and I was selfish enough to think of nothing else."

"Then my warning may be of use. Listen, Emanuel. If you loved this girl passionately, and hoped to marry her, you might possibly gain your wish; for I believe there is nothing her father would not in the end consent to for her sake. But I don't believe you could be happy with her, or she with you. She is a sweet loving child, with a child's feelings. She has, I think, no strength of character, no enduring, absorbing affection. Either she must lead a life with you to which she would be utterly unused—you know that she has never breathed our atmosphere of Bohemia—or you must live a kind of pensioner on her father, maintained as the husband whom his wilful and foolish daughter would marry, and who therefore must be taken into the family circle. You wince under this. Is it not true?"

"But there never was the faintest idea of anything of the kind. Never. Good heavens! one may speak to a young lady without—"

"Yes, one may; but when one meets the young lady very often clandestinely—"

"Clandestinely!"

"What other word can you find for it? Clandestinely, and nothing else. When one does this, he must contemplate something, or he must have no brains and heart at all; and you have both. Emanuel, I would, at almost any risk, save you from an entanglement that could only end, I am sure, in unhappiness. I speak to you, therefore, with an openness which perhaps wise people and good people would think does me little credit. Lilla Lyndon loves you!"

I am afraid the first emotion created in me by this declaration was a pang of fierce and wild delight. It was followed quickly, as by a rush of cold air on a burning forehead, by a chilling sense of hopelessness and pain and shame.

"It cannot be so, Christina; it is not so."

"It *is* so; I know it. Do you think I would talk of the poor girl so, if I did not know what I was saying? It is so. I have seen her lately; I know her well; I have talked with her many times; she has come and seen me here in this room; and a thousand things, a thousand words, have betrayed her poor little secret to me. Perhaps she does not know it herself. I don't suppose she has ever indulged much in examination of her own heart. What of that? I have eyes, and can see. If she were sinking into a consumption, she might not know it; but I should know it, or you. There is nothing much to wonder at in the matter, Emanuel. The poor girl has hardly ever met any men but elderly members of parliament, and heavy capitalists, and bishops. I know Mr. Lyndon too well to suppose he would allow any poor and handsome young curate ever to come near his daughter. *Wohlauf!* Your whole life is to her something interesting, strange, romantic. What is there to wonder at? I daresay if she had met a dove-eyed young clergyman in good time, the thing never would have happened. Mr. Lyndon is like the man in Æsop who shut up his son in a tower lest he should be killed by the lion; and, behold, the picture of a lion on the wall brought his death."

Christina spoke with flashing eyes, and with all the dramatic energy she always had shown since her girlhood, whenever she felt any interest in what she was saying. A stranger might have thought she was acting even now; but I knew she was not.

"Why do you tell me this—even if it be true?"

"Because I think I am speaking to a man of honour and spirit, and that the best appeal to you I can make is by the full frank truth."

"What would you have me do—supposing all this to be true?"

"Give up this girl—leave her—never see her again! Leave her before it be too late. She will forget you, Emanuel, believe me; she will forget you, if only you leave her in time; and she will marry somebody her father likes, and she will be a good obedient girl, and very happy, and her days will be long in the land, as the story-books put it, or the religious books, or what you will. And you will forget her; you say even now you do not actually love her. She will cry a little, perhaps; but all girls cry for something, and I really don't think it much matters for what."

"Christina, I don't like your tone—I don't like your way of speaking."

She laughed—a low, slight, scornful laugh.

"Not romantic and tender and sentimental enough, perhaps? But look what your romance and tenderness come to. You are teaching this girl to deceive her father—yes, you are;—yet you don't know that you love her, and you have no object whatever in meeting her! *Tarare!* You are not a boy, Emanuel, to act so any longer."

I bit my lips. I felt vexed and ashamed, and only too conscious that I deserved all she said or could say.

"Well, Christina, I must try to deserve your better opinion, and to act with more judgment and manliness. I make no promise, and I must act for myself in my own way; but I hope you shall have no further cause to feel ashamed for me."

"That is like yourself—your old self; I am sure you will do right after all. I would not talk to you in this way, if I thought you loved this girl; I would rather say, Fl'ng every thought away but that of loving her and holding her against the world. But you do not, and I think she will be cured at last of her love for you."

I rose to close the conversation.

"I will do my best, Christina. Existence, I suppose, is always to be a bore and a weariness and a renunciation to me. Well, I accept the situation; it will come to an end some time."

"O, pray, don't speak so."

"Yes; I am weary of everything. I am sick of this wretched profession—or art, or whatever you choose to call it—for which I have no heart and no genius, and in which I know I can never come to anything worth living for. I am tired of the people one meets, and the follies one commits, and the weary restraints one has to put on if he would not commit follies, and worse. What is one's motive in living? I don't know."

"Still we live, my dear; and we can but make the best of it. I at least will not see you sink away, Emanuel, into any folly or fatality without saying a word to interpose. Perhaps you think I have no right to preach or to advise?"

I waved my hand to repudiate this idea.

"But we made a pledge of friendship, Emanuel, when we entered on—that new chapter of

our lives; and I have kept it in my heart as sa-
credly as I could, though we have not often met.
And I do not—indeed, I do not—think this you
have done could come to any happiness for you or
for her. Perhaps I don't understand the little
girl quite, you will say," and she smiled slightly;
"but if I am wrong, the thing will come to pass
none the less because I ask you to be open and
manly, and yet careful. You ask me what is the
use of living, and how one is to bear with life?
My good friend, others have bitter burdens too
to bear, and bitter bad temptations to resist; and
I could tell you how they learn to do it, only I
dare not yet; you would smile at me, or think
me hypocritical, and I could not bear either.
But one time I will tell you—that, and other
things too, which now perhaps you do not know
or guess. No, don't ask for explanation; I have
said enough, and too much. Now, good-bye!"

END OF VOL. II.

LONDON:
RODSON AND SONS, PRINTERS, PANCRAS ROAD, N.W.